Works by Jack Fritscher

Novels

Castro Street Blues
Some Dance to Remember
The Geography of Women
What They Did to the Kid
Leather Blues

Non-Fiction

Profiles in Gay Courage: Leatherfolk, Arts, and Ideas
The Life and Times of the Legendary Larry Townsend
Gay Pioneers: How "Drummer" Shaped Gay Pop Culture
1965-1999
Gay San Francisco: Eyewitness Drummer
Mapplethorpe: Assault with a Deadly Camera
Popular Witchcraft: Straight from the Witches Mouth
Anton LaVey Speaks: The Canonical Interview
Love and Death in Tennessee Williams
When Malory Met Arthur: Camelot
Television Today

Short Fiction

Rainbow County
Corporal in Charge of Taking Care of Captain O'Malley
Stand by Your Man
Titanic: Forbidden Stories Hollywood Forgot
Stonewall: Stories of Gay Liberation
Sweet Embraceable You: Coffee House Stories

https://JackFritscher.com

CASTRO STREET BLUES

This *amuse-bouche* gay pop-culture novel of arts, ideas, and history, packed with comic dish, is a meta-fiction memoir told by a marvelously unreliable third-person narrator. The "coming-out novel" meets the "elder-exit novel" in the circle of life when the closet of quarantine disrupts a happily married couple aging in place.

The longtime husbands are survivors from 1950s homophobia to their rowdy post-Stonewall life of fifty years in San Francisco. Their pre-Covid queer life flashes by in homosurreal memory scenes of magical realism, gay travel, late-night movies, online cruising, and their own video-selfie diaries of friends gone with the wind of AIDS.

The author keeps this tale of lockdown, school bullies, wicked priests, body-image fascism, climate change, and gay marriage real and authentic with time-capsule headlines ripped from the news around MAGA insurrectionists, gay-bar shootings, and the migration of Black Leather Swans to Palm Springs.

"Jack Fritscher reads gloriously." *San Franscico Chronicle*

"Jack Fritscher writes wonderful books...careful writing...a world of insight." — Geoff Mains, *The Advocate*

"Jack Fritscher is an icon and pioneer provocateur from San Francisco's sexual heyday alongside sex idols Peter Berlin, Annie Sprinkle, David Steinberg, Rumi Missabu, and the Cockettes." —*San Francisco Magazine*

"Jack Fritscher is a prolific writer who since the late 1960s has documented the gay world and the changes it has undergone." —Willie Walker, founder, GLBT Historical Society, San Francisco

CASTRO STREET BLUES

A Covid Comedy
of Gay San Francisco

Jack Fritscher

A Popular Culture Novel

Palm Drive Publishing

For author history and for historical research
www.JackFritscher.com

This is a work of fiction. Names, characters, business, events and incidents are the products of the author's imagination. Any resemblance to actual persons, living or dead, or actual events is purely coincidental.

Cover Photo: ©2023 Terje Svendsen, terjephotography.com. Used with permission for all editions.
Cover and book design by Mark Hemry

Published by Palm Drive Publishing, Sebastopol CA
www.PalmDrivePublishing.com
Email: publisher@PalmDrivePublishing.com

Library of Congress Control Number: 2023937610
Fritscher, Jack 1939-
Castro Street Blues: / Jack Fritscher
p.cm

ISBN 978-1-890834-65-4 Print
ISBN 978-1-890834-66-1 eBook

1. Gay Fiction. 2. Gay History. 3. American Literature-20th Century. 4. Homosexuality. 5. Homomasculinity. 6. LGBTQ Gender Studies. 7. Popular Culture. 8. Covid Pandemic. 9. San Francisco.

First Printing 2023
10 9 8 7 6 5 4 3 2
PalmDrivePublishing™.com

Special thanks to my editor and husband
Mark Hemry

Epigraphs

Bliss was it in that dawn to be alive,
But to be young was very heaven!
—William Wordsworth, *The Prelude*

On or about December 1910,
human character changed.
I am not saying that one went out,
as one might into a garden,
and there saw that a rose had flowered…
The change was not sudden and definite like that.
But a change there was, nevertheless…
—Virginia Woolf,
"Mr. Bennett and Mrs. Brown"

So we beat on, boats against the current,
borne back ceaselessly into the past."
—F. Scott Fitzgerald, *The Great Gatsby*

FOREWORD

**Desperate Husbands
A Quantum Journal of Covid Quarantine
The Coming-Out Novel
Meets the Elder-Exit Novel**

Castro Street Blues. This fast-moving novel of gay San Francisco history is a meta-fangled fiction of passionate emotions told in flashbacks by a marvelously unreliable third-person narrator. It is an *amuse-bouche* gay pop-culture novel of arts and ideas. The coming-out novel meets the elder-exit novel.

The *faux* memoir, masked as a Covid journal, is a comedy of manners in which the observant author, writing in real time during the pandemic, deconstructs three years of quarantine disrupting the household of a married couple of gay elders aging in place.

As they try not to panic behind their masks, they feel increasingly invisible, turning eighty in isolation, taking refuge in books and films, seeking meaning in waiting, as one does, for a gay Godot to rescue them, even as they continue recording themselves in the video journal of selfies they have shot for forty years as Proof of Life.

The longtime husbands are representative men, survivors of gay history, from their coming out into the homophobia of the 1950s to their rowdy post-Stonewall life of fifty years in San Francisco before retiring to the Marin Headlands across the Golden Gate Bridge.

Quarantined there looking back at the iconic urban skyline, they watch online news of thousands of Covid refugees and renters fleeing the City, creating the most empty downtown in America, turning their once fabulous Castro gayborhood into a ghost town.

With the sinking feeling of drowning men, they see their pre-Covid queer life flashing before their eyes in slow-motion homosurreal memory scenes of magical realism, late-night *noir* films, teenage virgins coming out at schools and gyms and in the back row at the movies, gay marriage, and their own video diaries of friends gone with the wind of AIDS.

Having survived isolation in the closet and the viral AIDS years, the veterans of the midcentury gay liberation wars, surveying their personal history, struggle forward on their gay heroic journey through the dark cave of Covid vowing never to surrender to the PTSD many gay men carry from years of homophobia.

In his twentieth book, the author keeps this tale of Covid lockdown, the New Normal, and desperate husbands real and authentic with time-capsule headlines ripped from the news of the pandemic, the rise of MAGA fascism, guns and cameras and Harvey Milk, Saint Liza Minnelli, the great gay migration to Palm Springs, rainbow pronouns, and a transgender person leading the revived Pride Parade.

Director Oliver Stone said of his film *Platoon*, "This movie is not about me, but I had to be in Vietnam to write it."

If this literary fiction, packed with queer pop culture, seems as real as an autobiography, the author has done his job as an artist taking the reader on a fanciful ride as entertaining as his award-winning Lammy Finalist *Some Dance to Remember: A Memoir-Novel of San Francisco 1970-1982.*

Castro Street Blues

A Quantum Journal

1
A Day

Once upon a time fifty years after Stonewall, the old lord sat down at his computer in his suburban castle perched above Cascade Canyon on the rising slope of Mount Tamalpais. He looked out the panoramic glass window over his desk at his privileged CinemaScope view of San Francisco. The Bay was his moat. The Golden Gate his drawbridge. Across that flat sheet of sea surface, colored a beautiful blue-green by toxic algae blooming on discharges of treated water, rapacious billionaires drunk on hard cash erected skyscrapers so cocksure they stood like a row of rockets ready for launch in a space race of moguls shooting for the moon.

Tourists on Blue & Gold Bay Cruise boats pointed in awe and took pictures of the towering dark windows rising in hard verticals reflecting beams of light, down below, way down below, on the reclining soft female horizontal of the white skyline of ancient Victorians spread sensuously low across forty-eight rolling hills originally inhabited by the Ramaytush Ohlone peoples.

Channel 7 reported Millennium Tower at 686 million pounds was sinking one foot a year and leaning like a Tower of Pisa over the recumbent City. Water pipes breaking in the upper stories in the new tower at 33 Tehama flooded out hundreds of well-heeled condo owners who made suddenly homeless for months complained in English, Chinese,

Russian, Spanish, and Tagalog. As crime rates rose, the downtown shoreline — built on the mushy ruins of berthed Gold Rush ships scuttled by banks eager to make artificial fill to build more waterfront real estate — was slowly sinking around the entrepreneurs and the homeless and the queers into the rising waters of the Bay.

During the first year of the coronavirus quarantine, 58,764 people fled the City.

Extra! Extra! Headline News! Read all about it!
"San Francisco loses 150,000 office workers"
"San Francisco most empty downtown in U.S."
"S.F. 60,000 vacant homes during Covid homeless crisis"
"San Francisco high-rise windows shatter, fall to street"
"S.F. Mayor: Life as we knew it not coming back"

There was a pentecostal end-times madness upon the evacuees as if on the last day of the lost war in Vietnam, they were scrambling to get the last seat on the last chopper lifting off the roof of the American embassy in Saigon. What could possibly go wrong on the San Andreas Fault?

Cities breathe. Sometimes they inhale you. Sometimes they exhale you. Experience teaches wisdom. You may love the City. The City may not love you back. Not adjusted where you are, run down the moon. Go where your adjustment is, or just get out of Dodge, pack up, make your same mistakes in another city. Baudelaire warned, "The form of a city changes more quickly, alas! than the human heart." Paris grew tired of Hemingway's Lost Generation and took on new lovers.

2
Another Day

The old lord's landline rang out of the blue. It was a vintage pal, one of the fugitive kind, one of the last survivors of the witchhunts of the 1950s, the worst American decade to be gay. His caller, his fuckbuddy in the orgy years after Stonewall, had moved sag and saggage out of San Francisco to join the migratory flock of Black Leather Swans fleeing cities across the country to feather their retirement nest eggs in Palm Springs.

In his own Technicolor homosurreal dreams, he conjured his long-gone friends who were like him ripe old Lords of Leather from the last century. He imagined the surprise gift of their magical seniority casting a spell shapeshifting the leathermen into enchanted old ballet birds priapic with Viagra. He saw them, shades of Matthew Bourne, swanning *en pointe* across the blue lakes of resort pools with interlaced arms, grasped hands, heads tilted exactly to one side, one with a big fat cigar in his teeth, dancing as if they'd never been fisted the *pas de chats* of the "Danse des petites cygnes."

He himself was an ancient Black Leather Swan and he was starting to moult so he could no longer fly.

The voice on the phone picked up where they'd left off years before the pandemic. "You and your husband, good-old-what's-his name, should move here. Of course, you'd have to audition."

"Top? Or bottom?"

"It's a party town. Every hour on the Happy Half Hour some leather daddy turns seventy which is the new fifty. Under bar lights. If you squint."

"Spare me your stand-up comedy."

"Or it's wedding bells. Champagne cocktails. Two grooms on the cake."

"Don't come to the cabaret, oh chum."

"I'm making *beaucoup* tips at a little retro piano bar."

"The Plywood Room?"

"Singing show tunes."

"Singing swan songs."

"I'll have you know, I have a gazillion *likes* on Instagram."

"All from you?"

"Down here we're all vaxxed up fucking happy and happy fucking between boosters. I remember you when we were hot and you ran off with what's-his-name. Is he still hot? Are you still hot? I'm still hot. Has your face dropped? Why do you keep such strict quarantine?"

"Why do you live in a desert sucking up water for your pool?"

"I have a lovely green artificial lawn."

"Flocked with pink flamingos?"

"Camp like Divine!"

"Like a Bitch over troubled Waters."

"Said the man armies have marched over."

"Said the sodomite serving cocktails to the leather colony."

"I make a great Quarantini."

"What is it? Ketamine and poppers?"

"You have forest fires."

"You have tourists shooting obscene selfies up the skirt of that giant Marilyn Monroe statue."

"'Talk to me Harry Winston. Tell me all about it!'"

"That's *Gentlemen Prefer Blondes.*"

"Who wants a bitch with a *Seven Year Itch*?"

"Now I remember why we parted."

"Northern California is cold and it's damp"

"Humidity is my moisturizer."

"That's why the lady is a tramp."

"Who wants to die leaning into the curve of a grand piano singing show tunes?"

"My big finale is me in a big hat singing 'Don't Leave Your Heart and Other Body Parts in San Francisco.'"

"Must we have our own little culture war?"

"Maybe you're not gay enough in our Qmmunity."

"Maybe I'm way gayer than you think."

"On the Rainbow Spectrum?"

"Did you just make that up?"

"Are you still dragging that beard and ponytail pulled back for a cheap facelift?"

"The party's over."

"Now who's singing show tunes?"

"We do what we must and call it by the best name possible."

"Who said that? See how you are. You're always quoting somebody nobody's ever heard of. You're the queen of artificial intelligence."

"And you're a singing waiter nobody wants to hear."

"When I walk into a room it breaks into applause."

"When you walk into a room it breaks into flames."

"You are so bad in all the best ways. I love you."

"I love you too. See you in the funny papers."

"Next time let's Zoom again like we didn't last summer."

3
Six Weeks Later

Saying Goodbye to All That, he himself was old, pre-Stonewall old, working from a playbook of a bygone era, curating himself inside his gay apperceptive mass, born on the Summer Solstice three months before Hitler invaded Poland, emerging from the Art Deco gay past of the Before Time, swept from the 1930s into the 1940s and 1950s and 1960s meaning he was living in a kind of exile far downstream from his earlier life. Lot's wife leaving the boundaries of Sodom and Gomorrah looked back and turned into a pillar of salt that disappeared into the winds. He could turn back and look and survive. San Francisco was a city and a state of mind. He was an old man, an elder, with all the triggers that come with age. He thought he'd rather kill himself than live again through the first thirty years of his life before he moved to San Francisco, but assisted suicide was worse than assisted living which itself was suicide. So that was out.

The 1970s with afternoons on Castro Street and nights on Folsom Street was his gay heaven, the best years of his life, before the 1980s became a viral hell. He tried to meditate but all he manifested were sex fantasies. His appreciation of the arts began as a boy in a dark movie theater crushing on screen heroes revealing thrilling ways of being a man. The movies relieved the post-traumatic stress disorder gay men carry from early childhood growing up with chronic stress from living among mean girls and bully boys whose straight mouths and fists are assault weapons. Stress cleaned his arteries.

The Covid quarantine which was no retreat to Walden Pond was redundant to his isolation brought on by abandonment in the steady decline of relationships grown unsustainable by age, distance, and contagion. If Covid was hell, the quarantine of Covid Interruptus was a new season in hell, a purgatory, an insult added to injury to gay men who grew up isolated in closets not of their making.

People brag they like books. He actually read them. He re-read Thoreau who chose his two years of solitude to write *Walden* because he "wanted to live deep, Spartan-like, to drive life into a corner, and reduce it to its lowest terms."

As the fog of Covid rose in a grim remix of the horror of AIDS, he suffered withdrawal from his lovely addiction to friends and restaurants and galleries and theaters. He wore two masks and vowed he'd never elbow bump or fist bump if cornered into saying hello. Threatened by his senior vulnerability for almost three years he had seen no one but his doctor.

Television news showed old folks, old lords and old ladies, locked down in care homes putting the palms of their old hands like mimes flat against cold glass windows to touch the pressed palms of visiting loved ones standing outside in the snow. Thousands of people on ventilator breathing machines were dying alone in the hallways of overcrowded hospitals where idling ambulances polluting the air waited for hours in the driveways to deliver the dying and the dead. The homeless languished sick and ignored in sidewalk encampments where bodies lay suffering on cardboard. Outside hospitals, body bags piled up inside humming refrigerated trucks awaiting quick burials without funerals.

Every evening at eight during the first summer of the pandemic people in cities locked down around the world opened their windows applauding healthcare workers who were burning out. On Youtube, in Rome at eight, a local Pavarotti standing on his fourth-floor balcony sang "Nessun

Dorma" live over a backing track of orchestra and chorus to all the stranded neighbors in his apartment block applauding and shouting out their windows to each other over the empty streets *All'alba vincerò! Vincerò! Vincerò! I will win at dawn! I will win! I will win!"*

In Paris, a saxophonist high on the roof above the deserted Bears Den gay bar sent ribbons of Piaf's survivor's song "La Vie en rose" spiraling across the gay Marais to the open windows of lovers lonely in lockdown.

In Berlin, an ancient trumpeter standing alone in the window of his *Altbau* attic apartment sent a heartbreaking "Imagine" soaring to the moon over the Brandenburg Gate.

In San Francisco, a pair of dancing queens belting karaoke from their third-floor window across from the Castro Theater blasted out Sting and The Police singing "Don't Stand So Close to Me."

Had he, had everyone, had civilization done something wrong to deserve this? What? This punishment? Had circumstances and passions somehow compromised him? Was he drowning unable to breathe in a sunami of the surging scourge? Was the virus disrupting everything with extra stressors during the American madness of mass shootings?

The dead never die. He carried the trauma of Jack Kennedy dead, the first president he loved and voted for, shot by Lee Harvey Oswald shot by Jack Ruby before his very eyes on Live TV; of Andy Warhol shot by Valerie Solanas, SCUM-bag founder of the Society to Cut Up Men, two days before Robert Kennedy was shot by Sirhan Sirhan who bumped the wounded Warhol off the front pages; of Harvey Milk, the first gay man he voted for, shot by ex-cop Dan White.

Taking the veil, retreating into the first quarantine in the first twelve toxic weeks of 2020, he got them ol' Covid Blues. He had an anti-bucket list of things he'd never do again. With sixty-three mass murders since new year's day and trigger-happy cops and an orange sack of bully in the White House, he was still reeling from the slaughter of forty-nine queer folk and the wounding of fifty-three more at the Pulse nightclub in the repulsive state of Florida. He knew things had reached a pretty pass when the locked-down Eagle bar in San Francisco promised to re-open offering its hundreds of leathermen monthly Active Shooter Training.

"The NRA gun lobby won't quit," he told the Husband, "until it has a float in the Pride Parade selling Guns for Gays."

He thanked the Godz that whatever fate happened to him and the Husband would at least happen in San Francisco. The need for family roots was no match for the necessity of gay uprooting. They were immigrants who left everything they knew for a better life. To become your own person find your own people. As young men questing a hero's journey fifty years before Covid, they had fled the medieval Midwest because, rewilding gay masculinity, they wanted to live ten years in the future in California, light-years ahead of the dark patriarchal continent.

Could Covid quarantine emptying the streets calm the bloody gunfire, the car exhaust, and the virus? And maybe the wildfires? Nature recovers when people disappear. Covid fatigue waxed worse every day, every week, every year. People feeding on gas-station food and energy drinks stared into phones watching headline news and dancing cats, hardly noticing the evaporation of democracy while a chaos of lies, gunshots, and nationalism erupted around them. He lamented that the most dangerous persons in America were angry young white males, throwaways from trailer parks, graduates of the best reform schools, delinquents for rent in the talent pool of the irresistible grifters and drifters whose pent-up frustration and sex and violence gay men target with lust and disarm with cash and should never invite into their lovely homes. Wining and dining and blowing these Caliban manimals, Oscar Wilde said, was "like feasting with panthers." The risk was the excitement.

If all this armed and dangerous nightmare would ever end, he'd salute anyone left standing whether they survived by will power or luck. He had little interest in changing the self-talk of his inner monologue.

"I'm so fucking sick of this drought," he told the Husband, "I'd kill to walk in the rain. Two years of this pandemic, we've lost a year's worth of rain."

"You may get your wish. This just came up on my newsfeed. 'Atmospheric megastorm rivers of climate change increase chance of California megaflood in the next twenty years by 200-400%.'"

"So long, San Francisco."

4
Whan that Aprill

Floating on the raft of their queen-size bed, the old lord felt moored to a tiny island with one palm tree like a *New Yorker* cartoon, alone with the Husband, his very congruous spouse with long blond Buffalo Bill hair. Even within the satisfactions of their happy marriage, they missed their former life cruising out together into the wide world of variety they could never be to each other. He rolled out of bed and sat at his desk searching the internet for the self-care of erotic serotonin. His computer screen lit up like the wall in Plato's cave with a streaming imaginarium of men offering safe coping and solace. Cupid was in the air shooting digital arrows of voyeur sex.

It's a scientific fact among philosophers on gay bar stools that a lover can be everything except other people and that hydraulic tools must be pumped to keep up the pressure power of lift and loft and lunge. He knew the minute he allowed himself to feel the pandemic horror to its fullness, just as he had felt the crushing fullness of homophobia, he and the Husband would be swept away in despair.

He struck the space bar and was able by his Midas touch to make come alive every golden dream and sex fantasy of his adolescent desire. He had nineteen open tabs. His browsing algorithms led him to men and action and homomasculine visions he longed to see and even more exotic male things he'd never known existed and some made by artificial intelligence he wished he could unsee. With pot and the internet and a cock ring, he could go on forever.

He transcended isolation revisiting the *auld lang syne* of the he-festivals of his past when he and his friends had barnstormed every bar and bath from San Francisco to West Berlin to Tokyo to New York to Salt Lake City where they exited the Club Baths at 4 AM and the remaining five Mormon men exhausted by their reverse conversion therapy gave them a standing ovation. He found perverse *frisson* in the scary fact that if most gay fantasies came true, they'd be fascist nightmares like his hero Pasolini shooting movies about rough trade and then, as if his *Salo* came true, being murdered by teenage neo-fascists on the beach at Ostia where he and the Husband, taking the thirty-minute "Roma-Lido" train ride from station Piramide/Ostiense near the graves of Shelley and Keats, once spread a bouquet of blood-red roses across the sand on the shore of the Tyrrhenian Sea.

He inhaled then exhaled Walt Whitman singing of his own self, and every self, recounting male bacchanals and thousands of brave comrades cavorting "At he-festivals, with blackguard gibes, ironical license, bull-dances, drinking, laughter." He knew what Whitman knew. The rush of men, miners, 49ers, to the he-festival of San Francisco in 1849 never ended. The Gold Rush came out of the closet with successive new waves of bachelor pioneers, sailors, soldiers, ribbon clerks, ladyboys, and sex refugees rushing hellbent into the open City with its male brothels and bull-dances to live their best lives.

Judy Garland, the oracle who knew everything, made grown men cheer. *"San Francisco, you let no stranger wait outside your door."* He was eternally grateful to the City. In the 1970s when thousands of sex refugees of rainbow genders arrived seeking sanctuary, San Francisco opened its arms. In the 1980s when thousands of gay men fell ill, San Francisco opened its hospital doors. One night at the Brig bar on Folsom Street, his gang-bang of pals reckoned that when the 1960s and 1970s ended with AIDS in 1981, they'd balled untold legions of men, one-on-one and in orgies, but they laughed they hadn't cum with them all. He was as grateful for his sacred fucking in the Before Time as he was for his marriage.

He and the Husband had more weddings than Elizabeth Taylor, the queen of the marrying kind, wearing a flesh-colored skin-tight satin slip, holding a whiskey glass aloft, and standing poised like a lacquered cello all honeymoon lips and tits and hips leaning in a bedroom doorway in *Cat on a Hot Tin Roof* and *Butterfield 8*.

On the first day Vermont legalized Civil Unions, they arrived in Brattleboro to begin their journey to marriage equality by creating a legal paper trail of their political intent. The first week Canada permitted gay marriage, they wed in a Vancouver hotel witnessed by the chef and concierge arriving with champagne and cake to celebrate the hotel's first gay wedding. On the Valentine's weekend San Francisco suddenly issued licenses, they married in City Hall on the grand staircase crowded top to bottom for days with hundreds of brides and brides and grooms and grooms marrying and exiting outside to the front steps — where Dianne Feinstein had announced the death of Harvey Milk — feeling like movie stars greeted by applauding crowds handing single roses to the newlyweds. For four honeymoon weeks in San Francisco, they were husbands joined together until state courts put them asunder. Four years later, the California court reversed itself and they wed again on the Summer Solstice, for four months, until the fuckerie of the November vote on Proposition 8 banning same-sex marriage slapped the likes of them across the face.

At the height of Covid when the Trumpled Supreme Court overturned abortion and threatened to undo gay marriage, he went on a wild disruptive tear of new thinking in his journal. "Queers are divine. Homosexuality is a natural intuitive Old Religion predating the revealed religions of Druids, Jews, Christians, and Muslims." Falling on his knees to hear the angel voices, he invented his own old-time religion, re-setting homosexuality as an existential call, a natural spirituality protected like all the filthy-rich made-up mega-churches preaching junk theology in malls and issuing Certificates of Heterosexuality to their true believers.

His first vision of the sanctity of gay marriage had come to him, years before their many marriages, in *fin-de-siècle* Paris when he and the Husband fleeing the States over the hateful Defense of Marriage Act retreated for a month to the divine Hôtel Saint Germain on rue de Bac, boutique rooms nested in a mansion built in 1650, where the ancient Madame who had owned the place since Louis XIV was a child sat like a queen in the lobby keeping an eye on her young Algerian desk clerk and reminiscing to the ever-changing audience of curious tourists about the past and the drama of dealing with Nazi officers who occupied all her rooms.

Walking out of Madame's hotel into the warm evening of the Autumn equinox, they stumbled into an apparition of marriage when a singing procession of seven girls rose up out of the Metro entrance at Saint Placide busking their way to a bachelorette party in Montparnasse. Six of them wearing comic vestiges of wedding drag escorted the seventh, a young bride-to-be in jeans, veiled in a cloud of white, who was selling pieces of her mother's wedding veil to pay for her own trousseau. When he raised his video camera, the eager girls, one gone gaga for Dada with a penciled-on moustache, lighter than angels, giddy with fun, circled around them vamping for the money of the tourist lens, saying that sharing the veil brought everyone luck.

"Buy a piece. Buy a piece."

The Husband dug into his jeans and gave the bride way too many loose francs, and everyone laughed, and the seven girls, bride and six maids, seven sisters, cut two small pieces of net from her veil and gave them over, all of them singing into the camera, "Goin' to the chapel and we're gonna get married." It was an irony the happy hen party could not know. They were singing a battle-hymn to a couple struggling to marry. Off they ran with scissors into the brilliant Paris night, seeking centimes, leaving the old lord and the Husband changed, charged with new fire in their own wedding march, carrying in their wallets the veiled promise of their good-luck charms.

He wished his ancient high-school coach, the late Father O'Neill, the older wise-ass boys called Father O'Kneel, was alive so he could freak him out confessing he had a mystical vision of same-sex marriage as a gay sacrament. Gay boys are the wild card in the straight deck. God knows, back in the 1950s during the fear and anxiety of the McCarthy witch hunts against the twin menaces of red commies and lavender queers, the sly Irish priest, proud of his separatist celibacy with women, had tried to groom the teen lord's puberty into heterosexuality, but he could not be groomed by fascist dictates against his intuitive nature.

He knew nobody straight could ever teach him to be a man. He refused to dismiss his intuition. He was modern if they were not. "In this intuitive primacy of the Old Religion," he wrote, "lies the liberation of homosexuality through constitutional freedom of religion." Why not? With the traveling salvation shows of white Christian evangelists cashing in on fake religions on cable TV? With the *Deus ex Machina* of artificial intelligence creating gods? And Chat-GPT religions with AI preachers controlling sinners in the hands of an angry AI God? He had to hand it to the sexual outlaw Joseph Smith fabricating the Mormon doctrine of polygamy to justify to his screaming wife why their pretty young maid was his mistress. Why not a gay religion in a country where red-state religion claimed Trump was Lord and Jesus was his Prophet?

5

A Second October

From the night they met at Harvey Milk's birthday party, the Husband and he were boon companions, old souls,
good at remaining vivid to each other. If they had never
met in the 1970s, their lives on Castro may not have ended
in comedy. They thrived on the intuitive naked intimacies
that survive when blind gay passion becomes eye-opening
human love tender with privileges. During forty years, their
personal spaces blended into a safe mind meld. Each anticipated the other's comfort with little courtesies that brought
joy to their satisfied household. They couldn't believe their
luck. They lived inside their history as they had during
AIDS when sex became a blood sport like Russian roulette,
as they did every year during fire season which was now all
year, refreshing their two packed suitcases, their emergency
go-bags, clothes and food for them and the Border Collie,
waiting by the door.

Another April came a cropper, came in second as the
cruelest month, and gave way to October, unlucky October, the second Covid October, eighteen months into the
quarantine, seventy-eight thousand and two hundred and
twenty-four minutes into the pandemic, October, the most
dangerous month for fire, came again.

Drought again. Golden California sunlight, apple-crisp
mornings, ripening vineyard color, them biting their nails,
alert, awaiting calamity, fearful of the autumn aroma of
burning leaves, *alert*, sniffing for far-off brush fires, easterly
Diablo winds, lightning storms with no rain igniting golden
hillsides, flaming skies, smoky darkness, frantic escapes,

people perishing in homes where they slept, 190,000 people living around them in the wooded suburbs, evacuated, including them, leaving their home of forty years perhaps for the last time, *oh, what a sinking feeling*, running for their lives to shelters at Veterans Buildings, Covid super-spreaders teeming with pacing men, and women nesting with crying children on cots, and the confused wandering elderly bussed in from old-folks homes.

Distrusting the Covid protocols of pet-friendly hotels that for fifty miles around had no vacancies after the first wave of refugees, they slept homeless with their rescue dog for a week in their hybrid sedan pulled in at crowded evacuee parking lots, steeping a growing compassion for the unhoused, resolving to put more action behind their empathy.

The day that dry lightning ignited the firestorm, they escaped out of the wooded hills toward the freeway merging in with a rush of swerving cars, radio bulletins reporting alerts warning of panicked drivers speeding onto the freeways still racing away from their homes on forested back-country roads where they dodged animals on fire, dogs and horses and foxes running across the roadways, manes and tails spreading trails of orange sparks and flames through the dry fields and vineyards. In the town north of them, 2834 houses burned to the ground. Neighbors who couldn't flee jumped into swimming pools, huddling alongside small wild creatures diving in to save themselves, all of them dying of smoke inhalation. Disasters came like San Francisco MUNI buses: no sign of one for ages and then suddenly six arrive together.

"Wildlife population on planet declines 70% since 1970"
"Migrants drown crossing border"
"Covid cluster hits Provincetown vaxxed and unvaxxed"
"Global rainwater unsafe levels of forever chemicals"
"Orange president Space Force to colonize Red Planet"

"Four mass shootings per week in 2022"
"1 in 5 households buy guns citing pandemic chaos"
"Pope forgives all sins without confession til Covid ends"

Every single morning during the dirtbag presidency, the first thing he and the Husband said when they woke was, "What's he done now?" Trumplestiltskin, grabbing women like bowling balls, was spinning the fibre of democracy into webs of lies. Politics stronger than plague caused them to mask up and drive their mail-in ballots to the County Building to vote for Joe Biden carrying the torches of Jack and Bobby and Teddy Kennedy and Martin Luther King.

He enjoyed the vicarious natural human pleasure of watching life unfold upon others, without that someone, like Jay Gatsby or Sebastian Venable, having an awareness that someone besides God was watching him. Gay voyeurism is a factor of the closet where you can't be seen and all you can do is look. Boys who want to play must watch boys who won't let them play.

Some afternoons their security cameras recorded him as he slow-danced his nude Tai Chi to music in the secluded garden they planted as an outdoor library room with Walt Whitman lilacs, Robert Frost birch trees, Marlene Dietrich linden, Mapplethorpe calla lilies, and Faulkner roses for Emily sleeping with the gay dead. He moved and stretched and breathed to become one with the bodies and spirits of thousands of nude gay men of every look, one-spirited, two-spirited, trans-spirited, spirited away, too soon, too soon, dancing the divine melancholy of Satie's *Gymnopédies*.

He remembered his friends, the men disappearing from the surging streets, the juke-box bars, the jam-packed discos, the restaurants with empty chairs and empty tables, twice as many dead from AIDS than died in Vietnam, remembered them all, those sexy men, each and all sexy in their way, who came from everywhere living it up when

Beautiful People of all kinds of strange beauty, even the hot off-beat ones who looked like Picasso experimented, cruised the Titanic 1970s before the iceberg of AIDS. Beauty was their vocation. Some of them, some of his Folsom Street tricks, like the horse-hung young hippie stallion in the orgy room at the Barracks bathhouse whose thick blond braids he'd pulled back like reins, came so hot to his memory they materialized like glowing outlines of wire figures written in thin air by kids waving burning sparklers in the dark, like Cocteau's luminous lighting paintings, like Beatrice Lillie's fairies dancing at the bottom of their garden.

6
Another Summer

"What's cooking with you?" The Husband's voice called to the old lord on the intercom from the kitchen.

"I'm writing an email." He wasn't. The old lord was sitting in his Office of Good Intentions staring out his castle window at the red-bearded red-meat red-state redneck who lived next door with his obedient wife the man called Pancake. He was far different from those hot men the young lord had stared at out his window in the gay homeland of the Castro in San Francisco years before he and the Husband migrated across the Golden Gate Bridge. The neighbor's swaggering aggro type somehow perversely hot like all bad boys was suddenly popular as "MAGA Worship" on gay-porn fetish sites. It's all fun and games until an insurrection begins a coup.

With little else to shoot in the gunsite of his hidden video camera, he took to filming short clips of the bully-boy genius next door.

The Pomo Indians who once owned the land where he and the Husband colonized and gentrified and mowed the patch of lawn they bought, believed cameras stole souls. He certainly hoped so. His cock-eyed camera was his power tool to take reparations vengeance against all the bullies who owed him for stealing pieces of his soul. Like James Stewart housebound in *Rear Window*, he could not resist watching other people which is the essence of cinema.

As a boy, he learned from Father O'Kneel's jocks, and later from the A-Gays, that inside every secret fraternity was a more secret fraternity. He learned that inside every orgy of select guests fueled by pot and poppers and acid there was always a more select group sneaking off to the bathroom to shoot up with shared needles. They had died first. He liked adult sites with candid nude locker-room videos of grown men shot like Nature Channel cameras streaming the secret lives of animals.

He set up his tripod and aimed his camera out through the mini-blinds. He was more intentional than their wide-eyed security cameras staring at the neighbor whose security cameras aimed back at them in a world where cameras unmasking privacy were everywhere. What came first? The observer or the observed?

He turned his lens in fair play on the hunter who camouflaged himself to shoot deer with his AR-15 semiautomatic assault rifle that the man boasted shot blasts of adrenaline into his dick. Cameras were the new guns.

He felt like a voyeur in French films paying the brothel madam to peer through peep holes to watch bad-boy sex in the adjacent room, *Oh là là!*, the way men peered at men through gloryholes at freeway rest stops and at the underground toilets outside the front door of Notre Dame in Paris. "I have fifty francs. It's yours for a kiss." Cruising, killed by Covid and facial-recognition CCTV cameras, had been his joy. Shooting a stealth documentary of the handsome gunman next door was some kind of new Covid cruising.

Tens of thousands of years ago, multiple forms of humans shared the planet. The neigborhood chunk of locally-sourced Neanderthal still carrying genes for full body hair was one of them. He crossed the gay threshold of being so bad he was beyond camp. He busted his buttons joke-bragging to the old lord's Husband he got a DUI for driving an electric scooter into shelves inside Walmart. He crowed his pitbull was a pure purebred from a line of expensive purebreds. He thought it shucking hilarious he'd dropped his five-year-old off at the wrong school where no one knew him.

Late one night, drunk, standing at the redwood fence between their homes, he called to them sitting in their garden and bragged to the masked queers, baiting them twenty feet away, that he was a man's man goddam proud of his stamina. They choked back their laughter till later when they lay in bed imagining him stroking off in the mancave shed he built in his garden, dick in one hand, gun, they supposed, in the other, masturbating for hours to his recorded coverage of the pornographic January 6 attack on the Capital which he cheered on like an NFL football game.

"You don't say," they said.

He didn't ask and they didn't tell that many gay men fancying a kind of payback revenge for being sexually objectified as queers by straights jerk off to images of straight men turned into fetish sex objects by gay cameras that transubstantiate them into *objets d'art érotique*. With white masculinity, straight and gay, in crisis, he wondered if some straight and gay men were made for each other. If Holden Caulfield became a man by having sex with a black whore, did every gay man deserve at least one straight redneck served up *en brochette*? And vice versa.

They didn't tell him about the other neighbor, a husband who years before AIDS was door-bell trade. The guy showed up unannounced on their porch when he was horny, and they always welcomed him into their Stage Door Canteen for Desperate Husbands. Harvesting breeder seed to save the planet from the crush of another billion fucking people was their activist contribution to population control.

The gentleman caller, "Mr. Doorbell," fascinated them when he confided man-to-man, "Sex with you is cool because you're guys. If I had sex with a woman, I'd be unfaithful to my wife. I'd never commit adultery. I love my wife and kids. I know I can't fall in love with another man."

Again they choked back their laughter. When they explained that AIDS was not a gay disease, the dude cried and never returned.

Saving money under the mattress for a midnight ride to Washington on a Greyhound bus, the deerstalker next door was dangerous and hellbent on meeting his one coming big moment of disrupting the presidential election in 2024. "I'm gonna burn some shit down." He thought he was a religious man, but he was an idolator of guns demanding open-carry for nuclear weapons, a control freak voting against women's bodies and gay bodies and trans bodies to make America great again. "If Jesus had a gun, he'd never have been crucified."

"I'm coming to the kitchen," the old lord said into the intercom as he picked up the day's newspaper and walked down the hall into the bright room lit with a chandelier from the demolished Fox movie palace and hung with collectible cooking pots and antique pans they rarely used. "Headline news," he said. "'Russians bomb passenger train near Ukraine nuclear plant.'"

"We're an ugly species," the Husband said. "We should never be allowed to leave this planet."

"Not if the universe knows what's good for it."

"Here's another one. 'Baby hospitalized with monkey pox.'"

"And begs for peanuts and bananas."

It happened so fast, and they laughed so much in relief of their stress they couldn't speak for three minutes until finally the Husband said, "They'll never let us back into society." And then they laughed some more and so much that the little dog laughed to see such sport and jumped up, two legs on their legs, and licked their hands with wet kisses that made them laugh even more.

"So what do you want for supper?"

"Eggplant lasagna," he said.

All their Covid recipes came from the internet. Prep time 75 minutes. Bake at 400 for 20 minutes.

7

Another Winter Solstice

He took escapist refuge in the time-travel of art and literature because television and the internet may crash and burn and disappear forever. Print may be dead, but like the Rosetta Stone that needs no electricity, it's immortal. He remembered Blanche DuBois hopped on a streetcar named "Desire" and then transferred to a streetcar named "Cemeteries" before she got off at "Elysian Fields" where she blundered into her straight redneck brother-in-law who saw right through her. He wasn't sure about the existence of Elysian Fields, but he remembered Desire and knew the certainty of Cemeteries. He feared he might die leaving the Husband alone. He was terrified the Husband might die leaving him alone. He fell into a cliche of tears listening to Jacques Brel's "Ne me quitte pas" sung in gay San Francisco poet Rod McKuen's translation, "If You Go Away." He preferred them dying together in a garret in Paris, but what of their cremains?

What would happen to them if not entombed in the brilliant urban woods of Père-Lachaise near Oscar Wilde, Marcel Proust, Isadora Duncan, and Jim Morrison whose grave he lay down on full length among the roses and candles and love notes and empty whiskey bottles as the Husband shot video. Or near the pair of the handsome young balloonists of *La Belle Époque*? The two Frenchmen without masks, trying to ascend farther than anyone before, flew higher than Icarus into thin air and suffocated in sweet sleep in each other's arms, floating slowly down to earth, buried together in one tomb topped by a verdigris bronze sculpture of their two sleeping bodies, laid life-size side by side, arms and fingers entwined, fingers laced eternally, a hegemony of historians insisting they were straight, but what is straight existentially in Paris when two men die in each other's arms? For the old lord and the Husband every visit to the cemetery was a pilgrimage and on every visit they garlanded the cold bronze bodies with flowers that, so *Mrs. Dalloway*, they had bought themselves at Un Petit Fleuriste on Avenue Gambetta.

Like Leopold Bloom wandering through Dublin graveyards contemplating sexy re-writes of pious epitaphs on tombstones, they had a certain gay affinity for cemeteries the way some gay men are queer for theater organs and vintage railroad carriages. They socially distanced far from the madding crowd, hiking in a nearby country churchyard on the old lord's new hips and the Husband's new knees, walking their dog every day during a thousand days of quarantine, measuring on their pedometer more than two thousand miles on the peaceful garden paths of the pretty little cemetery and crematory where there were few visitors and everyone was six feet apart six feet under and the masked groundsmen waved and yelled, "Hola, amigos!"

When he felt he had to gin up a stress-cleansing cry, he watched animal rescue commercials playing sad music online under videos of frightened and shivering old dogs begging with tears in their eyes to be saved because nobody loved them. Weren't he and the Husband rescue gays from homophobia? He made himself misty watching Youtube shorts billed as "the most emotional moments ever caught on camera." Crying over random acts of kindness, he loved-hated his silly self weeping over a movie clip of young doomed enemy soldiers trading sweets and cigarettes and singing "Silent Night" in English and German across the muddy trenches of No Man's Land during the short midnight Christmas truce of 1914 when gaydar stronger than machine guns and mustard gas turned the hugs of young enemies who would die before dawn into erotic embraces.

One day, he and the Husband putting irony to Browning's bishop ordering his tomb at Saint Praxed's Church dared mask up and drive across the Golden Gate Bridge to Grace Cathedral founded during the Gold Rush, so like Notre Dame, so like Chartres, to buy their columbarium niche in the boutique Chapel of St. Francis, upper-left over the main altar and under the gothic Bell Tower, that would make them permanent San Franciscans. He liked that the Cathedral was Anglican embracing diversity because he was afraid their gay graves would be desecrated in a Catholic cemetery.

Should he fill his pockets with rocks and wade into San Francisco Bay the way Virginia Woolf loaded her pockets and took a long walk on a short pier into the River Ouse behind her house and drowned? Who's afraid of Virginia Woolf? The answer is "Virginia Woolf." Her famous room of one's own turned out to be the worst room of one's own depression. Eighty years before this plague in the spring of 1941 when the last two years of her life overlapped with the first two years of his, she could not keep calm and carry on faced with rising fascism and the coming rerun of the horrible First World War that like the first American Civil War had never really ended.

He was a man drowning in Covid whose life was flashing before his eyes from a movie projector reeling out of control tangling him in tentacles of octopus footage. Could he save himself in a room of his own? He could pack up their hybrid car and like a fool escaping to an appointment in Samarra drive till he ran out of power outside some desert shithole like Barstow where there were fake Iraqi villages to train soldiers he could ogle at the bar in the downtown Hotel Casa del Desierto.

8
A Summer

A thousand years before Covid in the summer of 1955 when he was sixteen facing his junior year in high school, he got down on his knees relieved he had one of the first injections of the new Salk polio vaccine in his arm boosted with a newer Sabin polio vaccine on a sugar cube. He was working the ice-cream counter at Meadow Brook Dairy scooping double-dip cones the summer before the September his teen idol James Dean died at twenty-four escaping he'd think years later the joys and sorrows of living past one's sell-by date. In that florescent-white sanitary-dairy store, his world changed. A desire unknown to him outed him to himself. It was his most shocking memory of his transition from a boy-with-a-parallel view of straight life to a gay boy-with-a-parallax homosurreal view of the universe.

He swooned when the first bodybuilder he ever saw in the flesh walked up tanned and shirtless in jeans to his counter and ordered a chocolate milkshake with three raw eggs. Straight men carry a spoor only gay men can smell. The man was every gladiator statue in his Latin book. He was afraid the older stronger teenage boys straight out of *Blackboard Jungle* constantly combing their slick ducktails and making a sport of pumping out biceps curls with heavy gallon glass jugs at the milk counter would notice his eyeballs had popped out of his head on springs and were bobbing up and down.

There had been a photo, "Steve Sales," in the *Evening Star* newspaper, an aspirational photo of him posing in Speedo briefs, "Mister Twin Lakes," a handsome beefcake armored with muscle, a picture of health, invincible health, long dead now of a heart attack at fifty. He had dared go to Sales Health Studio, "Step Back & Look At Yourself," 608 North Monroe, a vintage rack-and-stack gym with old-school iron barbells. He was about to learn the gay survivalist art of passing for straight to get what you want.

He needed the camouflage of muscle for self-defense against straight guys by learning to look like them so he could hang out with them and be strong in his own way. He wanted a man to teach him the command presence alpha males know from instinct perfected by lifting heavy weights that square a man's jaw. He studied them studying their manly look, posing in mirrors, pumping up, measuring themselves in pounds and inches, never operating outside their gender in a postwar world turning female.

He paid the bodybuilder, the first man he ever paid, five dollars out of his seventy-five cents an hour at the dairy — oh, how good the god's summer sweat had smelled — to coach a three-visit trial guiding him hands-on into the proper form and performance of lifting weights while he (hardening) furtively tingled to the man's hands-on touch (twice, just twice, chaste fingertips lifting the tips of his elbows) even while he carefully spied on three other shirtless young guys his virginal gaze was queering in the dozen mirrors on the walls.

Gyms are hotbeds of espionage. When the butts and backs and shoulders of the shirtless muscle boys left beads of crystal sweat puddling on the flat benches and the incline benches, he stripped to the waist and waited his turn to lower his bare back down like a thirsty sponge. He may not have known what he was doing, but he had a feeling he was doing it right.

When he asked "Mr. Twin Lakes" if he could film him with his father's 8mm movie camera, the man flattered to be asked said yes, he'd pose.

After the week, he never returned because he had bagged his movie footage and the men in the mirrors were glancing side-eye at him and one of them winked. Was it come-on or threat? In those glances, he sensed he was still just a boy, jailbait, yes, but he was sure he was the material out of which men are made and that was happiness. His father, his daddy, his Da, the straight wise-child farm boy who had seen how it was among the pairs of hired hands coming and going for lambing in March and haying in May and detasseling corn in July, gave him the Talk gay boys need.

"Be anyway you want to be. Your way in the world will be easier if you remember most people prefer masculine men in the best sense, not the worst. It's not fair, but sissies get hurt and I don't want my boy to be hurt."

He treasured that little Technicolor muscle movie the Husband had digitized. He kept the original reel inside the shoebox under his bed alongside the yellowed newspaper clipping, the photo of "Mr. Twin Lakes," the rosebud talisman of his spring awakening.

9
Week 110

Thirty years after that summer on his endless questing manhunt, the young lord becoming the old lord turning fifty and invisible once spent a week, seven fervent days of voyeurism, hiding in plain sight for 168 hours in Fresno shooting lawmen competing in the Police Olympics. With the queer eye of his observational camera of evidence and imagination, he transformed the rowdy three-ring sporting events into twenty choice hours of erotic framing and angles and ravenous closeups of a bold gay gaze no television sports network ever knew.

Among his sweeping takes of hundreds of wrestlers and boxers and bodybuilders and 250-pound powerlifters pumped with action, he held his breath for the divine moment of stillness, the perfect moment, the platonic ideal moment when he could focus his telephoto lens for two minutes to capture an ultra-slow video portrait of the face of a god standing still in the center of the action. Face is hotter than dick. Face is the essence of cinema. In New York at the Garrick Cinema in the 1960s, the young lord learned from Warhol films that a still portrait is lifeless compared to a pulsating video portrait.

His perversatility feeding on itself turned him on. Exercising his queen's gambit of acting up, he turned their competitive sports macho into eye candy. He didn't want to be assimilated and he didn't want to segregated. He lacked the toxicity of self-hatred. He figured the non-Catholic bad boys he coveted at Meadow Brook Dairy grew up to be hot men. He wasn't a gay heterophobe. He was fascinated by their mystique and the *frisson* of spying on them. He couldn't have them, but he could possess their images.

Remembering his father's advice about the cloak of masculinity, he was careful not to rouse any latent homophobia. He had shed the gay fragility of boyhood and didn't want to be sexually profiled. If gender performance were an Olympic sport scored on the Kinsey Scale, his quiet homomasculinity tied for gold medals with their loud heteromasculinity. Like an undercover cop, he made himself invisible behind his camera. A deputy sheriff seeing he was a man with a press pass doing his job pushed through the onstage crowd to bring him an A-frame step ladder so he could climb up above the scrum of encircling judges and referees and iron-plate loaders and spotters and shoot down on him and his buddies.

He zoomed in on their big bodies laid back flat in their skintight power-compression singlets on the bench-press platform. He shot fetish close-ups of chalked hands and exploding faces huffing and struggling to set new records. They never noticed or they didn't care that the silent photographer who did not interrupt their flow was gay. He *was* Ziegfield glorifying the American girl. In trade for making them even more beautiful than they were with his camera that made them immortal, he borrowed their souls and bodies, and turned their sports to gladiator porn so subtle the cops themselves could have watched without cringing.

He felt he was channeling Saint Genet in his Paris jail cell amusing himself composing his film *Un chant d'amour* filled with masturbating prisoners forced by guards to suck on guns with close-ups of bodies, armpits, penises, and faces trading cigarette smoke through straws in the walls between cells. On the other side of the wall of the solitary cell of his motel room, he could hear a small posse out of some of the hundreds of lawmen he shot by day getting drunk and loud by night.

While he eavesdropped, he took himself in hand for his first look at their guest appearances, their star turns, in the hours of raw footage he had shot that day. At least, he consoled himself, years and years before this Covid non-life, he had a parallax life among all those strapping young officers of the law who were now thirty-four years older and wondering what WTF happened. Straight folks cream over pictures of grandchildren. He and the Husband creamed over their bespoke cassettes of moustached cops and sweaty deputies and tattooed prison guards arrested by his queer eye in full athletic bloom forever. They were a comfort in their late-night Covid film festival that ended in tissues without tears.

At the end of the week, driving out of Fresno, he was pulled over by a young local cop who asked for identification.

"I want to see who you are," the cop said.

He handed him his license and his all-events press pass.

"I'm a photographer." He was relentless. "Can I take your picture?"

"Why?" the cop said.

"Why not? Tell me about yourself." That always seduced them.

"I'm a veteran. My war was Grenada. Five years ago."

They scanned each other. His dick was hard. Two looky-loo cars drove slowly by, and a motorcycle. He snapped three photos. But nothing happened.

"Have a nice day," the cop said. "Don't publish my picture."

"Thanks. It's for personal use."

Chasing bad boys was a risky turnon. He drove off shaking in his boots and hard in his pants. He laughed when he turned on his radio's oldies station and Mickey and Sylvia were singing "Love Is Strange," his favorite song from his senior year in high school.

"Are you still emailing?" The Husband's voice came through the wireless.

"I'm supposed to be writing in my journal, but I'm reading the headlines." He was doomscrolling a litany of disasters. Would the News ever run out of news? He could do a "Sing-Along with the Headlines."

"Trump claims election stolen"
"Global assaults on democracy"
"15 million global dead by Christmas 2021"
"Climate extinction crisis underway"
"2 million refugees cross Texas border in 2022"
"Greenland shedding 6 billion tons of water per day"
"Delhi hits 121 degrees, birds fall from sky"
"GOP ends abortion, vows to end gay marriage"
"Planet on fire, airports in chaos"
"Russians castrate Ukrainian soldiers"

He hated Russia.

"I don't want to interrupt," the Husband said, "but I'm ordering groceries."

"Listen to this," the old lord said walking into the kitchen. "'1830s Mississippi slave cabin listed as luxury Airbnb.' Perfect for weddings. Talk about playing the white privilege credit card."

"Let's play Covid Poker. I'll see you and raise you five bucks."

"I'll call you."

"Read it and weep." The Husband showed him the screen on his phone. "I have three of a kind. 'Cops say body washed up on beach is discarded sex doll.' And 'Girl 5 sobs learning she won't be a princess when she grows up.' And 'Long-Covid risk extends two years after infection.'"

"Hell is empty and all the devils are here."

"This wild card is even better." The Husband looked happy. "'Sex twice a week fights infection.'"

They begrudged keeping up with headlines but they didn't want to be like the two Japanese soldiers who held out for thirty years alone on a Pacific island because they didn't know the war had ended.

"What would the Futon-Duvets like to order tonight from Room Service? A bit of pâté?"

"I drink it all day."

"Let's make jam pennies like Queen Elizabeth eats every tea time."

10
Six Weeks After

Hoping to trick Covid into a late-in-life creative burst in his mindfulness journal, he treated the quarantine like an artist's retreat to distract himself and the Husband and try to make sense of their self-sentence to house arrest. Would people make art from Covid as they had with AIDS? He realized there was no plot to life. Life was a one-take series of scenes shot by a blind God who was a peeping tom with a hidden camera. Life was unreeling footage. Standup comedy. Standup tragedy. They joked they were "them," the alternative Futon-Duvets, wrapped in a gorgeous disaster movie like *The Garden of the Finzi-Continis*, so they made fun of themselves, stood outside themselves, imitating Dominique Sanda and Helmut Berger hiding from Nazis, playing at being two trapped characters in search of an authenticity in their buried life in their own private Garden of the Futon-Duvets.

What a pivotal jolt it was to their point of view in a time of rising militias of American stormtroopers bent on military occupation of the country to re-watch 1970s movies about the rise of fascism. Bertolucci's *Conformist*. Fellini's *Amarcord*. Visconti's *The Damned*. Pasolini's *Salò*. Fernando Arrabal's *Viva la Muerte*. Liliana Cavani's *The Night Porter*. Lena Wertmueller's *Seven Beauties*. Even Fosse's *Cabaret*. Especially Fosse's *Cabaret* starring Liza, the red menace with the green nail polish. They were shocked that period films about other people threatened by fascism suddenly seemed ripped from the headlines and terribly personal.

Late at night they tuned in and out of *noir* films of toxic men and toxic women on the classic movie channel, applauding the fierce Ida Lupino and the sneering-cool Robert Mitchum and the sneering-hot Steve Cochran who in real life died a hairy-chested corpse adrift for ten days on his yacht off the coast of Guatemala. For the first time, because they thought they should, they tried to watch vintage vixens of the kind men understand all too well like Bette Davis and Joan Crawford constantly impersonating themselves masked with cigarette smoke and rigid kabuki faces tricked out with no irony in their own pernicious drag.

Hitting pause, they said, "Queens like this? To each their own." And like a couple of swells being grand in white tie and tails in a Busby Berkeley musical, they said, "Let's call for Room Service," meaning they'd go to the kitchen and try to surprise themselves by hacking recipes.

"Pickled herring in wine sauce tonight, peanut butter and banana tomorrow, some smoked sockeye salmon, oatmeal made with green tea, Peruvian anchovies, and chocolate chip dough for the weekend. And hummus."

"I'll order online for delivery and say no substitutions and we can hope it's all in stock. The supply chain is broken."

"And then we can disinfect everything on the porch."

11
Years Before Tomorrow

There were detours on every road while he was changing keeping still in quarantine. His long-dead friend Thom Gunn, the man with night sweats, fleeing London for San Francisco, wrote a koan poem of enlightenment warning gay men must "dare a future from the taken route" because "one is always nearer by not keeping still." He clicked on his computer keyboard like a Magic 8-Ball seeking answers and maps for directions to an exit, any exit. He sneered at evangelical conversion therapists offering gays exits that were exit wounds because he knew there was no exit from the "'Hotel California' of Homosexuality" where in the song's Sartrean lyrics, you can check in, but you can never leave, and why would you want to?

If there were an exit, he could never abandon his queerness because it was the fountainhead of social empathy in his life that kept most gay men from being some fucking awful straight version of themselves, or worse, Log Cabin Republicans. Tennessee Williams said, "I am a deeper and warmer and kinder man for my deviations." He wasn't Garbo wanting to be alone. He didn't want to be alone. Can a man remix his life from closet to liberation to quarantine and back to society? Can a man survive hundreds of dead friends? Can anyone rescue an old dog with new tricks? He might as well have asked the search engine can a human born capable of love and trust survive when his heart turns to fear of others' hate and contagion?

He grew up in the heart of the heartless heartland where no one talked about depression. It was the denial of truth in that hometown that made truth so precious. He wasn't depressed they said. "All you have is low blood pressure," the first Doctor Quack said when he shot him up weekly with B-12 shots to buck up the skinny teenage young lord who was faint from wanting muscles. He was disappointed he had been born in a Midwest *Peyton Place* that was its own kind of quicksand where the village of idiots bragged I've lived here all my life because I'm a moron.

When he turned eighteen and graduated in 1957, he boarded his first airplane and escaped the pale of his hometown for a week in Greenwich Village where he dyed his hair red with spray from a can propelled by propane, butane, iso-butane, and hydrofluorocarbon 152a. He checked in clueless but suspicious and hopeful at the Sloane House YMCA on West 34th Street and hurried to watch *Wild Strawberries* at the Waverly Theater. He paid five dollars for his first Broadway ticket to see *Waiting for Godot* at the Ethel Barrymore. He bought yoga books illustrated with lean-sinewed yogis in tiny langota loincloths, and a pocket picture-magazine called *Tomorrow's Man* bulging with muscular young athletes in even tinier posing pouches "for artists who can't afford models." Not knowing what cruising was, he loitered like a tourist hick among teen beatniks playing folk songs around the fountain in Washington Square.

That night on a Murphy Bed in a downtown crash pad, a bearded young Michael rowed the young lord's boat ashore, spouting cum and poetry, doing to him what he had never had done to him before. "Like, it's Endsville, man, you dig?" Suddenly the shower room at the Sloane House made sense. Did the subtraction of virginity show in his face? Did he look different? The daughter of one of the morons said he was weird.

Keeping on the road like Kerouac, he was reborn in San Francisco in 1961 and in 2021 thanked what Godz there are, *Non, je ne regrette rien*, that he had lived the high life, *"inch by inch, mile by mile, man by man,"* every minute every hour in the 1960s and 1970s. When he first stepped off the *San Francisco Chief* at the Santa Fe Railway Station in the East Bay, Kennedy was president and the Midwest was 2500 miles in the past. He jumped on the Santa Fe bus-transfer connection across the Bay Bridge and felt his heart leap up at his first view of the City skyline shining with the golden light of afternoon. He stored his suitcase in a fifty-cent locker in the *moderne* Santa Fe Bus Passenger Terminal on 4th Street and walked fifteen minutes north through Chinatown to City Lights Bookstore. He knew San Francisco dreamed the way he dreamed.

To remember his face in that unforgettable moment of arrival in the City of his final destination, he sat alone behind a curtain in an automatic photo booth in North Beach posing for a filmstrip of four still frames. In those black-and-white selfies, he was wearing beatnik sunglasses, the boyish down of a chinstrap beard, and a knit shirt he'd bought from Parr of Arizona with its beefcake models in its *All-Male Mail-Order Catalog.*

He remembered how lucky he was the next afternoon standing hopefully in suit, shirt, and tie under the marquee of the sold-out Curran Theater when an older man of forty took pity on him who looked sixteen and offered him his extra matinee ticket to see Ethel Merman in *Gypsy.* Sitting ever so politely next to the man, second row center, he was overcome with surprise when Merman locked eyes with him across the footlights, pointed at him, and shouted, "My name's Rose! What's yours?"

"Are you alright?" the man whispered. "You're trembling." He was smiling. "Is this your first Broadway musical?"

The young lord suddenly fathomed how gay he really was.

"Welcome," the man said, "to San Francisco. Perhaps you'd care to join me for a little after-theater drink?"

12
New Year's Eve

On the third New Year's Eve of the pandemic, he told himself, Don't be depressed in your otherwise beautiful life. Depression is the worst room in the best hotel.

During the first Castro Street Fair on a hot August Sunday in 1974, the young lord survived a shooting at the corner of 18th and Castro that bummed him out and put his picture standing over the gunman's dead body on the front page of the *San Francisco Chronicle*.

"Fatal shot at Castro Street fair"

That sunny afternoon under the ticking clock of the Hibernia Bank cheers of fun welled up from the festive crowd of 5000 Castro clones, shirtless gym bodies, drag queens, lesbians, and leatherboys cramming shoulder to shoulder, cruising each other, browsing vendor booths, laughing, smoking pot, and moving to the beat of music from the bandstand set up for Sylvester near the marquee of the Castro Theater. The fair was Harvey Milk's brainchild to register new voters; but the City, snubbing the ambitious interloper from New York, refused to close the streets to stop cars from driving through the queer intersection packed curb-to-curb with a surging sea of people. Some of the crowd, led by two campy mimes and a cheerleading Cockette with a bullhorn, made spontaneous resistance a sport. For a few minutes of street theater, before the joke got old, they pressed hundreds of *faux* mime hands against the rolled-up car windows of a dozen bewildered drivers stalled to a standstill in the four crosswalks.

The young lord was just stepping into the jammed intersection near Donuts & Things when shots rang out. Buckshot richocetted off the Hibernia walls. Women fell wounded. The trapped crowd screamed with nowhere to run. An SFPD cop sprinting hard down the sidewalk, pushing and yelling, gun drawn, shoved him aside, knocked him down on his butt in front of a stalled car. Time stood still. People backed away from him and the cop and the fast-approaching shooter. Looking up in shock, the young lord saw the redheaded gunman blasting off another round, coming closer, stumbling. twisting, falling flat on his back across the hood of the stalled car. The man who looked so young got off another wild blast into the air before the cop jumped him, straddled his legs, leaned over his torso, and fired his .357 Magnum point blank into his ribcage six feet from the kneeling young lord's face.

The *Chronicle* reporter and cameraman covering the fair were suddenly covering a killing. "I didn't know how many shots he had left," the officer said. "I shot him close up for fear my bullet would go through him and hit someone else." Was it irony, coincidence, or fate that guns framed the brief four years between Harvey Milk's first real public event and his murder?

"My ears rang for a week," the old lord said. "I was traumatized." He kept the yellowed newspaper clipping inside the shoebox under his bed. "I was depressed for a month."

"I wish I'd known you then, my love."

"Suddenly, that summer, I realized the Castro was a mirage that could not last forever."

13
Another Day Like the Day Before Tomorrow

He felt as sorry for men who came out in the 1980s as he did for the aging millennials and the new Gen-Z kids born too late to understand the visceral wild first years of the sex revolution when the psychedelic 1960s exploded in a glitter bomb at the 1969 Stonewall riot, and gay character changed. That swinging decade of assassinations ended with the first men walking on the moon three weeks after Stonewall, Woodstock six weeks after, and Native Americans occupying Alcatraz in San Francisco Bay four months later.

"Homo nest raided, Queen Bees stinging mad"
"Melee near Sheridan Square follows action at bar"
"4 policemen hurt in 'Village' raid"
"Great Faggot Rebellion"
"Police rout 'Village' youths second night of riots"
"Gay Power comes to Sheridan Square"

He loved the first decade of gay renaissance in the 1970s the way Wordsworth romanced the first days of the French Revolution: "Bliss was it in that dawn to be alive, but to be young was very heaven!" One summer after the two of them reading Shakespeare at Christ Church, Oxford, the Husband videotaped him kneeling against the wrought-iron fence around Wordsworth's grave at Saint Oswald's church in the Lake District during one of their tours walking thousands of steps per day, getting marvelously lost in the streets and narrows of London, Dublin, Rome, Paris, and Amsterdam.

In West Berlin, the last summer West Berln existed before the Wall came down in November 1989, the two movie queens needing to vent that summer of raging AIDS deaths stood at midnight, camera running, acting out their *Cabaret* bucket list, waiting to scream under the arch of the elevated railroad bridge at Bleibtreustraße S-Bahnhof Savignyplatz where Fosse filmed Liza teaching Michael York threatened by Brownshirts to scream his stress away as a train screeched overhead intercut with shocking smash cuts of Nazi Stormtroopers beating people in the dark streets.

The next afternoon hoarse from laughing and screaming up at the roaring train, they stood on the busy Kurfürstendamm filming the ruins of the Kaiser Wilhelm Memorial Church, bombed by the Allies when the old lord was four, and kept as a reminder of the stupidity of war. What a shock when two young punks with spiked mohawks seeing Americans with a camera pushed in and screamed into their lens, "See what you did!"

The old lord said, "You started it."

And there it was. World War II all over again. Caught on camera.

Later, over pork knuckle of suckling pig at the Restaurant Bieberbau whose delicate figurative stucco work survived two wars, the Husband toasted the old lord: "*Vive la résistance!*"

Late nights the pair of Covid castaways from a sinking pleasure cruise escaped to an illusion of travel pulling up from Youtube to their giant television screen fabulously kinetic GoPro playlists of walking tours vicariously visiting cities emptied and made liminal and eerie by quarantine, new ways of seeing public spaces, what the world looks like without us, standing on teetering thresholds of changing norms and changing climate and lost civilizations, dragging viewers through the nostalgia and dread and romance of dark deserted streets.

They pulled up videos of Amsterdam's Red Light District and Dublin's Temple Bar nightlife closed for business; gorgeous tours of nighttime London strolling past shuttered chip shops and West End theaters dark from Covid and Harrod's with its bronze memorial to Diana and Dodi; midnight walks on rainy Paris streets past booksellers' padlocked kiosks along the Seine; curated tours of tiny drones flying slow inside the closed Louvre hovering in homage before the *Mona Lisa*, sweeping up the monumental Daru staircase toward *Winged Victory* from whose base and boat an eternal Audrey Hepburn forever floats down the stairs in Givenchy's red chiffon gown; dreamy twilight gondola excursions *senza passeggeri* roaming deserted Venice canals; kayak cruises down the drought-striken Danube past the resurfacing hulks of rusty Nazi warships; scenic train rides through the disappearing snows of the Swiss Alps in the carriages of the Paris-to-Venice Simplon Orient Express.

14
A Midnight

Aimez-vous Brahms? He played at feeling French the way queens do just to get out of his head in the house while he endured the bondage of isolation. Bondage isn't bondage until you want out. Listening over and over to the surging movie soundtrack of *Goodbye Again*, Goodbye Again to All That, the yearning adagio of the third movement of Brahms' *Symphony No. 3*, suitable soundtrack of loss, Paris nights, X-rated nights at Le Keller leather bar at 14 rue Keller, becoming one with Ingrid Bergman and Tony Perkins, he was a man evaporating, falling down, pulled up, music releasing pain, fingers clinging to the carpet, to the bushes, to the trees, defying the gravity of Covid, fingers clinging to the leaves of grass rooted in the lawn, trying not to float up and away until, no need for suicide, dead by age or virus or gun or fire or earthquake.

Alternating Brahms with Bach on the soundtrack from *Phaedra*, the film that would not let him go, Melina Mercouri and Tony/Tony/Tony Perkins fucking in front of a fireplace during a raging storm, Melina rasping "I give you milk and honey and you give me poison," with loss, trapped on the Greek island of Hydra, Tony, a closeted Hippolytus, doomed from the beginning, driving, screaming at Bach's *Toccata and Fugue for Organ in F Major*, driving speeding sailing off a sea cliff, the cliffs of Hydra, the actor, the lover of Tab Hunter, too sensitive to play a motherfucker, playing straight in his Aston Martin sports car, rocketing across the screen in a dying fall into the Aegean sea, like his doomed wife, the mother of his two sons, speeding low, streaking

466 miles per hour across the brilliant blue skyline of Manhattan crashing into the World Trade Center, the last of his Sheila, leaving only her turquoise wedding ring in the rubble the day the American Empire began to fall.

He rewound his life trying to dive back into that fainting feeling he got in 1961 in the Bryn Mawr movie theater during the Camelot of JFK, during those freezing dark Chicago winters when he was in graduate school, living alone, getting off the El train under the dark lamplight at the Bryn Mawr stop, descending the stairs to the street, trudging through snow toward the bright boxoffice of the popular neighborhood dream palace only steps away, queer with longing, defying danger, loving danger, rebellious with danger, hard with danger, coming out, again, and again. Every closeted gay man plays the virgin twenty times. Like an actor, he learned his part watching foreign films in the back row of the Bryn Mawr, Dirk Bogarde on screen a dangerous queen ominous in *The Servant*, while from the movie seat next to him a dangerous hand slid fingers into his pants, him twenty-two and ten-times-a-virgin, learning not to shout out at the climax of a handjob.

15
A Summer Morning in Winter

Covid slowed life down, but the digital days slipped by faster than calendar pages flying off the wall in an endless prison movie. He picked spring daffodils on Monday mowed the summer lawn on Tuesday raked the autumn leaves on Wednesday prayed for winter rain on Friday waited for spring budbreak in the vineyards on Saturday. Was this the whimper not the bang he had hoped for? He thanked the twin gay gods Eros and Priapus, the only gods he worshiped, that he was not that pulse-fluttering queen Richard Cory schooled in every grace who, spoiler alert, one calm summer night went home and put a bullet through his head.

He thought literature and films spoke in code about love and death and like a dress rehearsal of life how to live. He brooded over Eliot's *The Waste Land* written in the brutal aftermath of the Spanish flu, so California, so Palm Springs, with its desert world of sun-burnt drought, cracked rocks, parched lips, dry bones, and "dry sterile thunder without rain." The old lord in him understood Eliot's *cri de cœur*: "My nerves are bad tonight. Yes, bad. Stay with me...Think neither fear nor courage saves us. Unnatural vices are fathered by our heroism.... I will show you fear in a handful of dust." Freud named complexes after Greek dramas whose wisdom anticipated his Oedipus complex by centuries. He knew that without the safe frame of a theater proscenium arch, the action on stage would seem like scenes suitable for treatment in an asylum. Homer warned that the gods like politically-correct queens are capricious and quick to strike.

"How would Freud handle this pandemic?" he asked the Husband. Freud's daughter died pregnant in a city far from him during the Spanish flu epidemic when travel was forbidden and fifty million died. In quarantine, Freud buried his grief in work adding Thanatos to Eros, death to sex. He remembered a movie from the Bryn Mawr watching Maggie Smith years before *Downton Abbey* starring in *Love and Pain and the Whole Damn Thing*.

He buried himself alive in Emerson's "Self Reliance" which was helpful, Camus' *The Plague* which was not, and the original unedited tubercular version of *Look Homeward, Angel*. He could not finish Dafoe's novel of Robinson Crusoe shipwrecked on a desert island, or his bubonic *Journal of the Plague Year*.

"I don't know about Freud," the Husband said.

It was a summer morning in the second year of Covid. They were lazing with coffee on the deck in their garden finding pleasure in recalling the succession of three Border Collies they'd loved over forty years, invoking Molly and Daisy and Gracie as spirit guides, two chosen, one rescued, to bring female energy into their home because no home can thrive as a one-gender preserve. The Irish immigrant nun who had mentored him to protect him in high school in the 1950s was herself, Sister Brigid, a bit of a Druid priestess masked as a teaching Sister of Mercy who had once been a dispatcher with the Dublin police Gardaí. She was the only nun in the school and the nasty boys called her Sister Frigid not to her face, but to his. She opened him to the future of women's voices preparing him to hear Miss Clarkson, his graduate linguistics professor in the 1960s, spelling out the only truly ungendered third-person human pronoun is *they/their/them*. The Husband of forty-three years, younger by eleven years, was a stoic finding a quantum of solace against his own silent existential blues, against their Covid Blues, in the chapter and verse of Marcus Aurelius Antoninus.

"But I know about Marcus Aurelius," the Husband said. "He stared down a plague for the last dozen years of his life. Legions devastated. Villages emptied."

"What was it?"

"The Antonine Plague. Named after him."

"That doesn't seem fair."

"Probably a strain of small pox."

"Ended with a vaccine."

"Last week," the Husband read from his phone over eggs and the avocado toast he was eating sarcastically, "after seven hundred years, scientists revealed that the Black Death started in what is now Kyrgyzstan. It killed 75 million people."

"More coffee?"

"It's the granddaddy of all the plagues that have followed."

"Fuck the Tsars and SARS that spawned Covid."

"The more times you catch Covid, the sicker you're likely to get with each reinfection."

"Until you just fucking die."

You haven't lived they reminisced if you haven't cum with a cock in your mouth. Timid young men fainting at home in the closet wake up lucky kneeling in a gay bar under the supervision of two or three tough customers. Boyhood ends the day you suck your first dick, swallow your gay first communion, and become a man. Gay sex breaks taboos and erases boundaries of class and caste.

"The bad boys my parents warned me about became irresistible bait," the Husband said. "They had no clue they were stimulating my taste in men."

"Fuck down. Fuck somebody badder."

The old lord was grateful he had picked up some street smarts from the *nostalgie de la boue* gay men have covering the waterfront like Billie Holiday singing the blues. *Hi, Sailor! New in town?* The leather bars South of Market Street were fine fish bowls filled with eager gay men mostly white and bougie like him. He appreciated the safe clean-cut drawings of Tom of Finland, but he lusted for the dangerous raw men of Rex flopped hard on cots in SRO hotels.

He remembered his itch for adventures in unlabeled sex cruising on midnight streets through dive bars like the Old Crow on Market Street where roustabouts of different faces and races drilled a truth or two about men into gay boys with a wad of cash. In the 1970s when tunnel-boring machines dug up Market Street to build an underground subway three-stories deep for BART and MUNI trains, thousands of sandhogs came to the City at the same time thousands of men were arriving in the new gay *arrondissement* on Castro Street. The Market Street dig was the beginning of the end of old San Francisco.

The urban-planning promise of crowds of passengers rushing up to offices from the underground stations triggered the Manhattanization of new high rises and high finance breaking the skyline and the cost of living. It was a shock worse than the 1906 earthquake and fire. Perhaps it was a curse from the Native American skeleton disturbed by shovels after resting for five millennia buried deep near the Civic Center Station.

For years during the big dig, he had roamed the eerie tunnels mapping the tracks and half-built stations, interviewing the workers, and writing technical manuals for the MUNI Railway. He could still feel his Toyota Land Cruiser jeep bouncing on its shock absorbers as he rumbled slowly across the temporary plank roadbed of thousands of giant redwood timbers laid side by side rough as railroad ties covering the deep trench gashed down Market Street.

On shift changes, men climbed up from the Market Street tunnels chasing fun to the 6th Street gloryhole clubs and Tenderloin peep shows because queers, unlike hookers in a rush, paid cash and took their time. At the foot of

Market Street across from the Ferry Building in the upstairs rooms and showers of the Embarcadero YMCA where cars and trucks on the upper deck of the elevated freeway roared like a raceway twenty feet away from the open sixth-floor windows, workers met gays in scenes out of porn movies.

"The last time of anything has the poignancy of death itself." From Sister Brigid's extra reading for credit, he never forgot the lines in *A Tree Grows in Brooklyn*. "This that I see now...to see no more this way." Betty Smith's Irish wise-. child Francie had the soul of a romantic gay boy. "You grieve because you hadn't held it tighter when you had it every day."

He mourned saying goodbye to all that.

"Life sucks," he said.

"That's why we have the arts."

"What's next? A plane crash in the backyard?"

"Nope," the Husband said. "Prostatitis."

16
A Wednesday

In tonight's performance, the part of the old lord will be played. And not played. Period. End of sentence.

Interior. Home/Living Room. After midnight.

Run scene at sensuous speed. In your own time.

Stage directions: In the very dark room, the old lord looks up blinking from his bright computer screen, removes his earbuds, leans into the intercom, and speaks to the Husband.

Old Lord: Are you coming down from your office?

Husband: I'm over here.

Old Lord: What?

Husband: In the dark.

Old Lord: Where?

Husband: Over here on the couch.

Old Lord: How long have you been there?

Husband: Long enough.

Old Lord: I've been jerking off watching men.

Husband: I've been jerking off…filming you on my phone.

Pause. Six beats of mutual regard.

Old Lord: (Taking out phone) Now…we're…watching…each other.

Husband: I'm stoned.

Old Lord: I'm stoned. Jerking off…filming you filming me.

Husband: There's a pair of us. Don't tell.

Old Lord: Two old lovers stuck between two facing mirrors…

Husband: …curving off into infinity…
Old Lord: …growing smaller and smaller.
Husband: Mr. Futon?
Old Lord: Yes, Mr. Duvet?
Husband: The dog wants to go out.
Old Lord: Aaaand…scene!

He changed quarantine costumes like a constant dress parade of a play evolving from tight jeans and tighter leather to casually loose drag like the young Walt Whitman standing arm akimbo on the frontispiece of *Leaves of Grass*, open-throated linen shirt, broad-brimmed hat, and soft canvas trousers handy for hands hunting trouser snakes at Pfaff's beer cellar in Greenwich Village. In the six degrees of separation, Whitman slept with Edward Carpenter who slept with Gavin Arthur who slept with Dean Moriarty who slept with Allen Ginsberg who slept with Neal Cassady who slept with Thom Gunn who slept one glorious weekend with him and the Husband who slept with all the king's horses and all the king's men.

"After Covid, Alzheimer risk increases 50-80%"
"Older men warned testosterone is fetilizer for cancer"

17
The Second August

His brain and heart were a cinema montage of everything he'd read. He had been so successful a student in school he could not stop studying. He tried to take on homework that warded off every senior's fear of dementia. Personality cannot be replaced. He challenged his rigid beliefs that were making his elder-world small the way being in the closet those boyhood years ago kept his world from opening up and out. Enlightenment crumbles untruth away. Turning the pages of *Against Nature*, he loved Joris-Karl Huysmans isolating himself dripping with lust for cherry-lipped youth while infecting Oscar Wilde and Dorian Gray. He remembered how Oscar nursing Bosie sick with influenza caught the flu from his faithless lover who did not return the favor the way lovers took care during AIDS.

He felt his mania for Huysmans's divine carnality evolving joyously beyond Huysmans the way Sally Bowles' agency for divine decadence evolved beyond her creator, Herr Issyvoo. *"You have to understand the way I am, mein Herr!"* After all those glorious years ago, escaping the Catholic isolation of his first eighteen years, playing at low-life fifty years ago in the 1970s at the height of his vigor, thirty-five, standing almost six feet in Harley biker boots, 150 fit pounds, riding dirt bikes, cruising gay bars, hitting gyms, wrestling rough sex, slumming through back-alley dive bars and sex clubs and gloryholes and other sloppy hell holes dripping with cum, he laughed at himself disinfecting groceries delivered to their porch by a millennial in a mask. Death was coming COD, but he didn't know how it would be delivered.

What if he could not wake up from this nightmare of plague that was no dream, as he had during polio and AIDS?

"Pandemic causes polio resurgence"

He was a porous person full of empty spaces absorbing everything. This was not the first virus to distance him from friends in his Rolodex who withered and died during the last twenty plague years of the last century. Oh, how he longed for the dear dead bygone days when it was still a thrill and a wonder and a victory to sit in a coffee klatch at the Castro Café listening to pals saying, "I sucked twelve cocks at the back of the Jaguar bookstore this afternoon and I've got two dates tonight." If only promiscuity had been a natural vaccine creating herd immunity. All those poor boys gone before they could heal the homophobic wounds of childhood and adolescence.

Lying on his fainting couch feigning *La Dame aux Camélias*, he coughed and embraced his life, getting older, keeping mindful, pulling to himself the spirits of his friends denied the gift of old age, trying to enjoy in his life the life they were denied. He felt for the new Covid Generation of kids waiting for vaccines, missing school, freaking out more than their parents could ever know just as he had freaked waiting for the polio vaccine.

In his panic, he had the heart of a hummingbird pumping 1200 beats per minute, ten times the beat of disco. With Covid, every headache was brain cancer. Every hangnail meant amputation. He had more drama than the motherless Prince William, the boy who would be king, the balding boy he admired, juggling his drama queens, his merry wives of Windsor, his indestructible grandmother and his father's second wife and his own wife and her mother and sister, quietly distancing from his rogue brother with his woke wife. The old lord was in his forties when Lady Di produced two princes spun from sperm sorted for gender in a centrifuge. He was hot for redheaded Harry, the bad boy who couldn't stop spinning, and he fancied Meghan who nailed the key of gay resistance when she described her husband and self and mixed-race children: "Just by existing, we were upsetting the dynamic of the hierarchy."

Having translated Cicero line-by-line in high-school Latin class in musty books illustrated with photos of nude statues of gladiators and soldiers, he thought it might be as glamorous as a Hollywood epic like *Quo Vadis* or *Doctor Zhivago* to live during the fall of a civilization. Be careful what you wish for. He never dreamed his eyewitness life would run in sync with the slow-motion fall of the American empire.

"Trump demands new election in bizarre overnight post"
"Man cured of HIV after stem cell transplant"
"Archeologists find carved Roman dildo at Hadrian's Wall"
"Woman sets fire to Pride Flag outside NY restaurant"
"Politically correct rewrite Roald Dahl's kids books"
"Drag Queen Story Hour becomes battle over gender"
"Red state challenges to LGBTQ rights highest in years"

He had cracked open his closet door during the deadly 1950s conformity of flat tops stiffened with the cum of Butch Wax, narrow ties, and oxblood wingtip Oxfords in his hometown bar, the Quench Room, gay code for what could not be called the Queer Room or the Queen Room without scaring the horses of the lumpen white city patriarchs who declared the Quench Room off-limits to local university students and announced to the *Evening Star* that nice people never talk about sex, politics, or religion because that kind of mansplaining censorship was how they procreated power in their top-down moral purifications.

There was no GoPro walking tour of that damned village of the damned morons. A *cri de queer cynisme* made the old lord smile remembering how embracing what we fear in order to survive we walk about like the spies straights suspect we are shooting mental pictures without a camera to photocopy bad boys into our late-night spank banks. He loved nothing better than a roaring ten-inch pound of flesh for sale at a hundred bucks a pound.

He figured anyone who rode the unbridled horses of the Merry-Go-Round up and down in the 1970s ought to be immune forever to any virus. But they weren't. Was he? Was the Husband? The AIDS virus had passed over their house. Maybe their retreat was wrong. Maybe you change nothing by isolating. Maybe "one is" indeed "always nearer" to the heart of life "by not keeping still." Maybe you just fucking spit in the wind and dare to ride out a pandemic on the painted pony you rode in on, but he was unhorsed like an old lord trying to joust on a kiddie carousel.

How do you justify taking risks? In twenty-three decisive minutes, passengers straight and gay who fought back on 9/11 hadn't just died when they crashed their plane down into a Pennsylvania field, they had disappeared at 600 mph in a ball of fire vaporized by seven thousand gallons of jet fuel. Is it better to be fighting in acute terror for twenty-three minutes on a plane or sitting with a Starbucks Venti intent on a computer in the twin Towers of Babel and not see it coming? Maybe twenty-three minutes is a minimalist blessing like three hours on the cross versus three months on a Covid ventilator or three years in quarantine. First thing each morning, they read their digital thermometer and their fingertip pulse oxymeter ordered in a panic from Amazon. A jump from a window of a high rise is not suicide if you make a parachute out of the curtains.

18
Day 1095

In the third year of quarantine, could anyone do anything that was safe or not contradicted or canceled in a world of inequality polluted from the oceans to outer space?

"Earth's inner core stops turning, reverses itself"
"Chunk of Sun breaks off, stuns astronomers"

Can't go to a restaurant? Can you eat take-away? The Futon-Duvets swabbed their grocery packages and jars with disinfectant wipes. They soaked fresh vegetables in one part vinegar and three parts water. They cooked every meal to safe internal temperatures. Half a lifetime ago at the dawn of AIDS when he asked his doctor in San Francisco about climbing into a hot tub at the baths, the new young Doctor Quack who shot him up every six weeks in the 1970s with anti-viral gamma globulin said, "Go ahead. Jump in if you want to be part of the experiment." That put the brakes on their public sex life. For four agonizing years, gay men presumed they were all fated to die until the HIV antibody tests began in 1985. Yet here he was forty years later even more erotically distanced from the world of strangers, still horny, untouched but for his sweet lover, turning eighty-three which was only 4330 short weeks of life. "Going once. Going twice. Do I hear 5000?"

The drowning suicide of abstinence made him a voyeur as his life flashed before his eyes. Seeking reassurance that homosexuality had not died and that the world of men had not disappeared, he clicked for company on the glass shield of the computer screen seeking haptic porn seances with athletic gods fluent in sex looking directly into the camera and speaking the salvific words lifeguards say to the drowning resisting their own rescue. He did not need prayer or meditation or online Sunday Mass from Grace Cathedral because the most divine moment of the day was the lightning flash of orgasm.

Most often when he clicked on his laptop, it was not for sex as much as for proof that out there existed a new breed of younglings he didn't need to film because like the Futon-Duvets they were filming themselves. Christopher Isherwood, an eyewitness voyeur of rising fascism in 1930s Berlin, said, "I am a camera with its shutter open... recording the man shaving at the window opposite." Herr Issyvoo could not see the scope of the cell-phone future. I am a camera? Everyone is a camera. Cameras were the Eyes of Harvey Milk. His Castro Camera shop liberated the gay gaze of thousands of cameras developing pictures of rainbow life straight camera stores refused to print. The old lord watched the gay pornsites where women could be thankful to God there were no women, where virile sex and heroic endurance still existed in a mad mad mad world armed with nuclear warheads.

He longed for the *auld lang syne* when the Castronauts brunching in the Norse Cove Café bragged the morning after the night before about combing their teeth. But those days of originality and passion weren't all phone numbers, kumquats, and sunglasses.

"Remember how we all cruised before cameras and Covid ended street cruising?" he asked the Husband. "And had to decide if we were going to fuck each other or kill each other?"

"The ones you don't fuck always hate you."

"So do the ones you fuck."

"I only fucked the ones nice enough to hold still," the Husband said.

"Every gay bar in the world is closed."

"That's a first. Call the *Guinness Book of Records*."

In the gay-lib decade after Stonewall, the Castro shimmered like a divine disco in a snow globe full of whirling rainbow glitter. So what if American guns were shooting in Vietnam and a man firing a shotgun into the crowd at the first Castro Street Fair was shot to death by a cop and homophobic orange-juice queen Anita Bryant was reigning over Florida, the septic tank of America. Everything was peace and love and granola fairy-dusted with sex and drugs and music up to the shocking minute Harvey Milk gunned down by an ex-cop reminded revelers gay men die. "Oh! thought Clarissa," in Virginia Woolf's *Mrs. Dalloway*, "in the middle of my party here's death." The cold night of the dark day Milk bled out from five gunshots on the floor of City Hall thousands of the thirty thousand silent mourners carrying candles in the sad funeral march led by a single drum down Market Street were dead men walking. Thirty months later, AIDS hit the headlines on the newspaper kiosk in front of the Star Pharmacy at 18th and Castro.

"Rare cancer seen in 41 homosexuals"
"Gay plague instills fear, no one is safe"
"AIDS is the wrath of God says Vicar"
"AIDS mom grateful 'embarrassment is gone'"

Some hot Covid nights, he checked in on his laptop to the Castro Live Cam streaming down like the sad eye of a distant God watching the dark street lit with a lavender glow from the Castro Theater marquee reading "Stay Healthy and Safe. We'll Be Back Soon." He welled with sorrow seeing the plate-glass aquarium windows of the Twin Peaks bar boarded with plywood tagged "Black Lives Matter," occasional "24-Divisadero" buses, airbrakes sneezing, passing in a slow cruise for lost riders, sidewalks empty, a masked Latina cleaner hurrying home alone, a ghost town even at midnight on Saturdays when the first founding bars once spilled acid-rock music and hot hippies come to San Francisco with flowers in their hair, and crewcut leather-men, and Castro clones, and screaming gay boys out the doors into the street.

He loved rolling on his tongue the litany of the pub crawl from the Pendulum and Toad Hall and Nothing Special to the Midnight Sun and Bear Hollow. The Castro in Covid was at the point of extinction. Every week small quirky businesses and landmark bars like Harvey's at 18th and Castro died into empty storefronts. Even the gay Cathedral of the Castro Theater was under threat from developers ignoring its hundred-year history shaped by fifty years of gay provenance. The friendly neighborhood pot pushers in the long-ago street party turned into ugly meth dealers after the Castronauts' exodus to Palm Springs.

Squeezed out of the Tenderloin, abandoned street people camped on the Castro sidewalks and held out white Styrofoam cups begging for spare change. Is there such a thing as spare change? Unhoused queer folk told the television news they felt safer sleeping encamped in the neighborhood of their identity.

Back in the day, he had flown higher than Icarus and the Parisian balloonists and David Bowie falling to earth where waves of claustrophobia surfed in foaming over him like a King Tide in the Bay. In front of mirrors, he stripped off all his clothes looking for himself in the *Vitruvian Man* algorithms of his body and face. The Black Leather Swan put on his vintage leather boots and leather chaps and leather codpiece and leather shirt and leather vest and leather cap and took them off and put them on. They fit his body but not his fantasy. Performing male agonies, he was like one of those ridiculous Civil War re-enactors trying to conjure what was gone with the wind. He pulled on a black suit and tie on Sundays and 32x30 blue jeans on Wednesdays and red Speedo briefs on Fridays and laughed at himself for being so lame on tanktop Saturdays, and told himself to go brush and floss because he feared the face-to-face intimacy of a dental cleaning.

He wasn't depressed. He was exhausted from living a perpetual Lent. What could a Covid zombie do to raise himself from the living dead and put himself back on sunny hiking trails? He stood up. He tried to shake off his endless sitting that was killing his stamina by trying to walk thousands of steps a day. He was dying by inches and ounces. Dear God, what's happening to me? "Come quick and kiss me now in a world gone mad." The old lord began to realize his life story had a beginning, a middle, and an endpoint that had no end and no point.

Unlike AIDS, Covid didn't beatify anyone into a martyr-saint. A body doesn't last forever. Would he ever dance again? All these years later, he still felt knee-capped by long-dead schoolboys who had wrestled and played ball sports and targeted him with wicked names that made everything else he was disappear like a stage magician's rabbit. *Poof! You're invisible! Poof, you're invisible!* His father, sensitive to the boy, giving his son a reason to cut sports, found him an after-school job as a paperboy with the local *Evening Star.* He worked alone making his rounds in rain and heat and the early dark of snowy nights as the only employed thirteen-year-old in the seventh grade, beginning a career, his father kidded him, in journalism as a newsboy carrying his own paper route delivering the headlines of 1953 door to door to a hundred and twenty houses.

"Stalin on deathbed after stroke"
"Queen Elizabeth II of Great Britain crowned"
"Korean War ends"
"Atomic spies Julius, Ethel Rosenberg executed"

"Eartha Kitt 'C'est Si Bon' tops Hit Parade"
"Salk gives self and his family the polio vaccine"
"Bob Hope hosts first televised Academy Awards"
"Eisenhower Order 10450 bans homos in gov't jobs"
"McCarthy HUAC hunts Hollywood Communists"

He was a paperboy who lay awake at night, every night, as he had since he was seven on the edge of his little bed wondering how he'd ever fit into the world whose depressing news he carried in a canvas bag heavy with forty pounds of folded newspapers slung across his aching shoulders, years before old Doctor Quack asked if he knew he was born with a touch of scoliosis, while his parents who loved their golden altar boy played cards, having fun at the dining room table, not able to hear him in the bedroom repeating, *nobody loves me*, over and over, *nobody loves me*, like a boy in an orphanage or an old man in a care home, *nobody loves me*, sliding on his belly slowly down the soft cotton folds of his Roy Rogers bedspread to the floor, *nobody loves me*, landing in a sweet ecstasy of sticky gaykid eros whose consolation he would not understand exactly until years later when he was fucked like a willing human sacrifice into a divine epiphany sliding slick in a snowy slalom of Crisco down the sheets of a bunk at the baths.

19
Half Past High Noon

"First I was a boy and then I was gay. I never became a man."

The Husband said, "Oh, stop!"

"What are you doing after lunch?"

"Paying the bills."

Oscar Wilde said, "Never love anyone who treats you like you're ordinary." His heart leapt up with gratitude. The Husband managed them so well. Their little dog loved them. Alone together they were the happiest they'd ever been in their fortunate lives. Everytime their skin touched, their happiness paused his sorrow as stars fell around them. He who did not drink or smoke felt drunkish and imagined lighting up a big fat cigar like Jack Kennedy winning the Cuban Missile Crisis. He felt he was in the best room of the best hotel. They were all three in the same room together and that was everything. He felt the kind of joy winners feel at award ceremonies. He didn't feel eightysomething. He had lived in ten decades and two millennia, but he felt fifty riding high in the saddle. He felt happy. So when he spoke his next words, his voice sang out, dropped an octave, and surprised him: "I love you, Honey. Thank you for everything."

"Are we prisoners of love?"

"Our own private Stockholm syndrome?"

"Our 'Homo on the Range.'"

"'Where never was heard a discouraging word.'"

"If this plague doesn't end soon, may Zeus fuck Poseidon."

"And go to Hades."

Six months. Ten months. Christmas. Easter. Halloween. Thanksgiving. To hash-mark time, they double-dared themselves to retro-watch one episode of *Peyton Place* re-runs per night. They lasted through 240 nights of the 514 Youtube episodes until even with hate-watching they couldn't take it anymore. Christmas again. Pandemic binge reading.

What did you do during the war, Daddy?

He nose-dived into big books living inside them, as Rilke advised, like a college senior cramming for finals in an English class. January. *One Hundred Years of Solitude.* Valentine's Day. *James Baldwin: Novels and Stories.* Saint Patrick's Day. *Portrait of the Artist as a Young Man.* He *was* Stephen Dedalus. On the southern tip of Dublin Bay in the shadow of Joyce's Martello tower, he and the Husband with their hidden video camera had stretched nude on the rocks at Forty Foot, the swimming spot in Sandycove, where for three hundred years pale Irish men with cocks white as perch have dived naked into the cold Irish Sea scooped out by ancient glaciers. April Fools. He stopped reading *Crime and Punishment* when Ukraine begged the world to boycott Russian novels because life expectancy on the front lines in Bakhmut was four hours. May Day! May Day! *Native Son.* June Pride. *The Well of Loneliness.* Summer Solstice again. *Death in Venice.* July fireworks. Hanya Yanagihara's *A Little Life.* Labor Day. *Middlemarch.* (Her name was Mary Ann and she called herself Marion but everyone knew her as George.) Schools closed for a second year. Durrell's *Alexandria Quartet.* Autumn equinox. Farrell's *Studs Lonigan.* Was he Studs, the Irish-American wannabe tough guy shedding Catholicism and struggling to be a man? Circadian rhythms. Halloween canceled. *Young Törless.* He *was* young Törless. Winter again. *The Proust Screenplay: A la Recherche du Temps Perdu* by Harold Pinter revealing "time that was lost is found and fixed forever in art." Spring again. He tried *Marienbad My Love,* the world's longest novel, with its narrator stranded still typing his endless book on a desert island. Summer again. He re-read the pages of *Gone with the Wind* in an edition prefaced with a warning of racial triggers, but all he saw in his head was the movie. He *was* Scarlett O'Hara.

In the third year of solitude when an assassin stabbed Salman Rushdie in the eye, he read his third-person memoir of survival *Joseph Anton*. What is time? What is quantum time? What is before and after? What are always and never? Is time sacred or profane? Is love timeless or fleeting? Can the mind bend time? Will Covid's disruption of time end in a nightmare of global jet lag? Over and over on his phone, he played the Eagles' "Wasted Time," a romantic melancholy in 4/4 time sung to an old desperado wondering as the days rushed on if they had all loved the boys too much or too well in the best years of their lives on Castro that was the Garden of Paradise before the Fall when they found no shame in their nakedness.

In 2022, on the second New Year's Day beginning the third year of the endless pandemic with a million Americans dead as viruses mutated, he sat down at his computer to start the new year in his mindfulness journal. He typed in his first sentence, "The old lord sat down at his computer." Was that him anymore? He quickly deleted *lord* and typed in *fool*. He felt marooned searching online for a note in a bottle he hoped to find floating toward him, washed up, stranded on his desert island like Amelia Earhart, where he'd spelled out SOS with palm fronds and rocks and seashells on the sandy beach of Omicron, hoping boatloads of sailors might row to his rescue.

20
Vespers at Dusk

Saint Derek Jarman canonized by the Sisters of Perpetual Indulgence masked with white face told gay men, "Film your life." For years he filmed the Husband with their video camera, but rarely himself. He was afraid he'd leave a stain on the screen. An online guru explained brains are wired to resist the way our faces look on video because we think we look like we look in mirrors. He had come to terms with his mirror image, but he cringed from his video face that seemed so off from what he believed was true in his mirror-mirror on the wall. FaceTime was out of the question.

He had no treatment but retreat for the wound that wouldn't heal from the bruising body-fascism in high school when the Midwest Catholic boys informed him he was a fag before he knew it. He confessed the pain of his shunning to the old-school priest, Father O'Kneel, the varsity coach he could not quit, a Marine sergeant in the World War, who scolded the unwilling sacrificial victim.

"You're not confessing. You're tattling. The way you think it is may not be the way it is at all. You're a liar and liars go to hell."

He feared being mocked and beaten up for being the teacher's pet, too bookish, too sissy, too sassy, too smart. The priest was a man's man.

"Your father should knock the corners off you. Wise you up. Look at you. Sit up straight. Stomach in. Chest out. Uncross your arms. Uncross your legs. Spread your knees."

He didn't want to sit up straight. It wasn't their business or his fault he preferred Grace Kelly to Marilyn Monroe, and Pat Boone to Elvis, and wore white bucks. He curled up in his bed listening to his 45rpm records of Grace singing "True Love" and Pat crooning "Once I Had a Secret Love." It was his business not theirs that alone in his room playing "Secret Love" over and over, he ached with hot burning puppy love and tears of anguish for his best friend shipped out of school with no goodbyes because, the priests announced, the seventeen-year-old "sissy caught with a copy of *Catcher in the Rye*" — borrowed on the down-low from the young lord — "had a 'nervous breakdown' and no student should ever contact him or his parents again under pain of being expelled and shipped out after him."

"At least, you're tall," Father O'Kneel said. "Jesus was six feet tall."

Their bully pulpit tried to silence him. Such abuse could tempt altar boys like him to sin a boy's worst sin against purity, the mortal sin of masturbation, the magical thinking of masturbation, the self-repair of masturbation, wallowing in male masochism, coping, turning the body and blood of gay pain into the soul and divinity of orgasm. Some boys held hostage by their humiliation grow so sexually addicted to their morose delectations they fall in love with the healing shame that makes their cocks hard, wacking off like sex martyrs in sweet surrender to images of alpha men who will fuck them up. Evelyn Waugh knew the invincible spin of perversity. His Anthony Blanche snapped at rich Oxford bullies who wanted to throw him in a river: "Nothing would give me greater pleasure than to be manhandled by you meaty boys. It would be ecstasy of the naughtiest kind."

In the spring when he was fifteen, a clique of older boys, students preparing for the priesthood, a cadre of Ku Klux Katlickers more Catholic than the Inquisition, pushed him backwards over a boy crouched down on hands and knees behind him and broke his fuck finger. Father O'Kneel clipping the end of a cigar said, "Suck it up. Did the priests in Dachau complain when stripped, beaten, crowned with barbed wire, and crucified? You'd make some man a good wife. Maybe it's time you should read *How to Win Friends and Influence People.*"

He tried to forgive them by meditating on the nearly naked muscular Jesus nailed on the cross hanging over the altar in the school chapel, but Jesus and his six percent body fat kept dissolving into the hottest of the boys crucified naked and hanging cross-fit to a T-square over the main altar in a bulging snow-white jockstrap.

Oh what a bucket list of suffering succotash to be crucified on Live TV hanging naked on a cross haloed in a pin spot of blue light. Religious sex fantasies always made him squirm. A little bit. The young lord found strength in the conjure power of religious fetishes like the "Crown of Thorns" displayed in Sainte-Chapelle where years later the old lord and the Husband sat for so many evening concerts of Vivaldi and Brahms. The way resurrection canceled Christ's crucifixion, his erections conquered his suffering. The way medieval monks adored crucifixion nails for their magic, he loved the abracadabra of his jockstrap. Catholicism depends on the casuistry of how you ask questions. The priest wasn't a Jesuit, but when a boy asked, "Can I smoke while praying," he answered, "No," and when a boy asked, "Can I pray while smoking," he said, "Yes."

"Every boy," Father O'Kneel said, quoting from the *Gospel of Saint Butch*, "should be an *alter Christus*, another Christ." The priest peered at him and asked a shocking question. "When you draw naked boys, do you draw them with or without a hardon?"

He was an inexperienced virgin, but some latent gaydar defense system made him cool. He saw the trap of the trick question. There was a third answer. He said, "I don't draw pictures of naked boys." It was the truth.

The priest sucked his cigar so hard the red tip crackled.

"Liars go to hell."

In that Autumn when he was seventeen, another scrum of jocks aroused during a cider-and-cigar night listening to sports on Father O'Kneel's enormous Wood-Cabinet Philco Radio plotted their vigilante punishment of him for threatening their gender. In a homophobic blood sport disguised inside the action of a friendly touch-football game, the apostles of masculinity knocked him down in the cold November mud and kicked out his front teeth because a heterosexual male's worst nightmare is turning gay overnight.

When you're gay, life isn't impossible. It's just harder. He would have died of defeat if Sister Brigid whose priest-brother had died young had not taken him under her wing. Her doctorate gave her power over the priests. She taught him what he did not know then was the queen's gambit he'd use all his life to defend himself. He took control.

Gay men have superpowers beyond the ken of straight men. Learning the intuitive invert strategies of deviance in high school, he spent a revenge year alone in secret, a senior at eighteen, pushing his tongue against the permanent dental bridge in his mouth, writing a musical-comedy with parts for all fifty boys in the glee club; but he played no part himself, would never go on stage where a posture or gesture he could not control might betray him to an auditorium of boys turning what every boy whispered about him into words that could be shouted in cat calls from the cheap seats.

Warding off the evil eye of pubescent bullies, he stirred up a potion of revenge served hot that would have made Hamlet hard. He sweet-talked the director of the glee club, Father Polistina, into casting all the hottest straight boys. Polly had the power to interrupt their ball games and draft them into weeks of rehearsals to say and sing the words he put in their mouths while his 8mm movie camera filmed them, fearful of their own inner sissies, tripping through what he told them was gymnastic choreography. When the opening-night audience of the one-night-only performance called out "Author! Author!" he dared take the final curtain call and bowed from the waist over the hardon doing a standing ovation in his pants.

That spring, Sister Brigid gave him her dead brother's copy of James Joyce's *Ulysses*, condemned by the Church as excrement of the mind for Catholic radicals, launching him into the beauty of its stream-of-consciousness, characters floating in scenes needing crib-sheets, half-remembered songs, tabloid headlines, quips on the quirks of Catholicism, masturbation monologues like Molly Bloom Herself unpunctuated saying *yes* and *yes* and *yes* like Sister Brigid Herself.

In 1957 with his father's camera, he took two days to shoot a four-minute silent movie picturing his noisy family in a composite series of scenes and angles his Mam and Da thought so funny they set up their projector and screen and chairs and folding TV-tray tables and invited the next-door neighbors over for their son's movie night. In college in 1960, he fell for Godard the way Godard fell for Joyce who owned the first silent-movie theater in Dublin, sitting in the projection booth while odd bits of non-sequitur images and title cards with dialogue patched into his fertile brain as he wrote cinematic drafts of *Ulysses* in the flickering dark. "When I close my eyes, Joyce said, "I see a cinematograph going on and on and it brings back to my memory things I had almost forgotten."

"13 September 2022, Godard dies, assisted suicide"

The old lord when he was a young undergraduate lord watching *Breathless* at the Bryn Mawr immediately understood Godard's handheld camera breaking Hollywood grammar with jump-cuts mixing hand-held action scenes with student-café musings about film. "To me life is just part of films," Godard said. "Movies should have a beginning, a middle, and an end, but not in that order." When the VCR arrived at the same time as HIV in 1981, he and the Husband, figuring they'd all die and gay civilization would be lost, began building their discontinuous video journal maybe ten hours a year for forty years.

"Warhol's *Empire*," the old lord said, "was seven hours of the Empire State building doing nothing. One shot of one thing."

"We can do better than that."

Their journal clocking gay life from the onset of AIDS turned into a mini-series of Covid disaster shock.

"Cinema" Godard said, "is truth twenty-four times a second."

"The unfilmed life," the Husband said, "is not worth living."

Shooting their endless video selfie helped them track and memorize themselves against the mind's sleep and forgetting the way he regretted no one could really picture the glorious past of the Golden Age in San Francisco when a camera before AIDS and the VCR could empty a gay bar because cameras were the guns of vice squads.

"Look," he said to the Husband, "what we always say finally hit the headlines: 'Virtual reality reminiscence therapy lets seniors relive the past.'" The footage their camera shot was their *madeleine de Proust*. He told the Husband, "If I get Covid brain fog, set me down to watch our lives."

Not every day, but some days when it hit them as the sun pushed golden beams of Vermeer light, the kind Proust loved, across the maple floor of a darkish room, brightening the green of a Boston fern, or the honeyed bow arms of a Stickley Morris chair, one or the other would shoot one or two minutes of the evanescent moment or themselves — the Husband was very photogenic — or their dog

or the neighbors or guests filmed back in the Before Time
arriving in their driveway for one of the famous picnics in
the Garden of the Futon-Duvets, digital ghosts all long
gone, mixed with quick insert clips of world headlines shot
from television and computer screens giving context to their
quarantine.

"Covid cases surge in unvaccinated"
"Climate fire burns 1000s of CA acres"
"Jury sees George Floyd say 'I Can't Breathe' 27 times"
"Rain on Greenland ice first time in recorded history"
"Gavin Newsom wins landslide against Republican recall"
"Biden Afghanistan exit worth chaos"
"Generals feared Trump would use nukes in last days"
"During Capitol riot, China believed attack imminent"
"Iran executes gay rapper for warring against God"
"Ice shelf size of Manhattan collapses in Antarctica"
"Putin's panicked officials' secret bid to end war"
"Shooter kills 10 Blacks at supermarket in Buffalo"
"Chinese accuse Dior of cultural appropriation"
"Number of lonely single men on rise"

It always took months of just grabbing the video camera
the way you always remember to grab your phone to fill two-
hour discs with the streaming montage that some nights escaping to the Before Time they viewed for the comfort rush.
Dunking their *Petit-Beurre* biscuits into steeping teacups of
calming elderflower, hawthorn, and Shakespeare's rosemary
for remembrance, they watched mediated moments of their
past selves talking to their present selves. The sweet pain and
bitter pleasure of immersive nostalgia hurt so good they felt
alive. They tried to kid themselves it was okay there was no
going back to the way things were.

"Maybe happiness," the Husband said, "is knowing
when you've had enough."

21
Pistols at Dawn

Their troublesome MAGA neighbor next door, a bricklayer denying the Holocaust, climate change, and vaccines was a caution about the inadequacies of fake patriotism. He may have been a man of his times seeing his kind on Fox News, a social terrorist feeding on lies and disrupting the public good, but he should have known better. Marching down a path of chaos, talking secession, poaching democracy, fighting mask mandates, he whittled his political beliefs to a sharp-stick obsession over God, guns, and sex. Hating gun control, he wanted government control of female bodies and gay bodies. The man's pronouns were *me/me/me*. How do you say *twunt* in English? He worshiped the orange wrecking ball. He suffered from Trump Persecution Syndrome. Everyone was out to get him.

He called the old lord a faggot.

The old lord called him a MAGAT, and stunned him for a moment with, "Two words. One finger, bud."

They both laughed.

"Now," said the old lord on a roll, "Let''s talk about habitat degradation."

The original exterior of the fucker's Craftsman bungalow the faggots called MAGA-LEGO suited the charming neighborhood, but inside it was fatally renovated.

"Brain-eating amoeba starving to death in red states"
"Right-wing anti-vaxxers are killing Republicans"
"Blue-collar jobs boost male fertility"
"14 shot, wounded at memorial for shooting victim"

The June after the January 6 attack on the Capital in the second year of quarantine when the neighbor yelled for all to hear that his $3000 purebred dog had goddam died, the old lord keeping it real turned on his hidden camera, watching from his window as the man carried his stiff Rottweiler into the yard where Frau Pancake who bragged about her breast milk smoothies, and his three pure purebred children from a line of pure purebreds, Hansel and Gretel and little Donald, stood at attention holding a Confederate flag.

Aiming his zoom lens like a gay Navy Seal sniper from behind Roman shades and Venetian blinds, he watched the man in the red baseball cap dig the grave when the man, quite marvelously, stood up in the shallow hole, picked up the dog's corpse, raised it up to Jesus, and keeled over in a seizure half in and half out on the edge of the grave and died, foaming at the mouth in a fentanyl death pose, with his dead dog in his arms.

Cue Liza. *"Bye Bye, mein lieber Herr!"* Life is a fucking cabaret. It was *America's Funniest Home Video*. Covid and politics had skimmed the milk of human kindness. It was not the win he wanted, but it was a win nevertheless. He dialed 911 for help. He *was* Abe Zapruder whose 8mm silent camera was the only camera filming the mind-blowing moment Kennedy was shot in Dallas. He remembered how he and the Husband had scored the lucky afternoon on the Mall in London on Remembrance Day in 1991 when riding into the viewfinder of their video camera came the Queen and Charles and Diana driving slowly by, three agendas with faces uplit by floor lights in the back seat. Watching his candid reconnaissance footage the night of the day the neighbor died in the name of his orange lord and savior, he found pleasure and anger there was one less white nationalist fool to abandon morals to support a contagious pig who was his own kind of plague.

To celebrate, he got as hippie high as Gertrude Stein munching Alice B's brownie delivered by Uber from his local village Pot-isserie dispensary. Buzzed and baked, he was delighted, sprung with joy, made young again, when he heard shouting outside their front window and never too blissed to turn on his camera, he called the Husband and shot two minutes of a dozen naked art students from the college, boys and girls, celebrating midsummer, streaking down the street running and laughing and yelling at the full Covid moon through their masks.

22
Time Lapses

"Whatever you do during quarantine," the old lord said, "don't count the days. It's always Friday. Then it's the week-end which is just two more weekdays that seem like four days." He wandered room to room cleaning and dusting what was clean and dustless. He told the Husband as long as they could keep their Covid safehouse *immaculate* or *spotlessly clean* or *clean* or *clean enough* or just *effing sanitary*, they would never need to retire to eldercare. He knew the pandemic would end but not in his lifetime. He was fading away. The hole in the *Titanic* was only three inches wide but it was a hundred yards long. So what hope was there in herd immunity?

His Covid weight dropped below his wrestling weight in high school where he won every match he lost flat on his back to tougher boys making them feel morally superior in their singlets plopping their conquering butts down on his chest, pressing him into the mat, straight thighs straddling his face, grinning down their sweaty torsos at him grinning back like Br'er Rabbit because he had maneuvered their succulent crotches into position under his chin where tucked in looking up he had the best camera angle in the world.

The late-show comedians joked about Covid weight gain. He had no Covid weight gain. He was Irish and carried the famine in his bones, in his genes always feeling hungry, starving, eating small amounts, living a perpetual Lent, his metabolism racing. Thin he was and thinner he grew. He was shrinking into Kafka's hunger artist who became useless to the circus when his anorexic starvation act in the freak show bored the spectators while Kafka himself, the master of self-flagellation, had a hunger for running his tongue up the long legs of blond Swedish boys.

Old queens never die; they just fade away. He and the Husband who was the fair grandson of blond Cornishmen from the fishing village of St. Ives were in their fifteenth year of the Mediterranean Diet starving for carbs. He stood naked and dripping wet in his steamy bathroom mirror where an old man stood in his way. He knew he was old the shocking day he sat on the toilet and tea-bagged the water. He had faced this destiny since he was thirty when Neil Young reminded an old man — the evaporating old lord all young lords become — to find joy in the reverie that he was once young: "Old man, look at my life. I'm a lot like you were."

He was a casualty of his own reflection, but unlike Narcissus he could not fall in love through a glass darkly with a face he could not recognize as himself. So he didn't drown. He had wanted to be one of those rangy old men still playing tennis and trimming trees in his eighties, but he looked like the ghost of the ghost of Lytton Strachey, the Victorian Stick figure bullied at school for his spindly physique, living the last sixteen years of his queer life writing in retreat with his adoring Carrington at Ham Spray House. He *was* Lytton Strachey.

In years past in the leather-fetish bars on Folsom Street, he had sported a big Harley biker beard full like Lytton's and Walt Whitman's and ZZ Top's, the kind it takes two years to grow, which he wrapped around cocks for extra thrills, but shaved off so Covid masks would fit his face. The pandemic ruptured the past. The old way of living and writing about our past lives, he thought, especially men's lives, gay men's lives, will no longer do, needs to be re-thought, in the Covid wars around drag queens, transgender liberation, and #MeToo activists.

This disaster was not what he expected for the last chapter of the charmed life he finally felt free to write and film the way he wanted like an existential examination of conscience. He tried to be honest. He'd never in his life thrown a queen's silk scarf over a bedside lamp. It was a wake-up call. He no longer had all the time in the world. Not to be undone by Covid, he could at least be creative and grateful. The old lord began to write in his journal about the young lord in the third person. He wasn't alone. He loved the Husband who loved him. They were one and the same.

Baudelaire, romancing dread, said, "I have cultivated my hysteria with pleasure and terror." He hadn't chosen his fate, but he figured he'd better embrace it. "Laddie, lie near me. Your dance class leaves at dawn." How enjoyable to sit and think with Lytton in his lap whispering, "If death is like leaving a party, it will be as terrible as the dreadful moment when one has to leave one's beloved. An agony, long foreseen." He could not bear the thought of leaving the Husband.

Faced with this shit, he decided to pull up his socks and get on with it. Free will trumps fate until gravity sucks and all fall down. To breathe one more breath, people jump from burning high rises. How do you hold onto life you can't bear to leave? Even if it's in Palm Springs with Doctor Silicone fattening competition penises like pigs in a blanket. He thought twice about the hope and glory of all the camp movie lines gay men quote chapter and verse like sacred gay texts and about the show tunes sung around pianos like gay hymns of climbing every mountain and walking on through the rain though your dreams be tossed and blown over the rainbow.

In the disco rhythms of his beat/beaten/beating heart, Gloria Gaynor was on a loop at the bottom of their garden singing "I Shall Survive" to the ghosts of dancing boys who would never take up tango and rumba-line dancing at the senior center. The wild-hearted Zorba the Greek, he remembered from the Bryn Mawr, asked the uptight student Alan Bates who could not dance, "Why do the young die? Why does anybody die? What's the use of all your damn books if they can't answer that?"

"They tell me," the gay Bates said, "about the agony of men who can't answer questions like yours."

"I love you," The Husband said. "Snap out of it. I'm searching to find a second booster shot, but we might have quite a wait."

23
June 2022

Like the crack of doom, after thirty months of quarantine, thirteen days after the school shooting in Uvalde, Texas, of eighteen children and two teachers that cops with guns could not rescue, the penny dropped. He came out into Covid. Waves crashed on shore. Trains rushed into tunnels. Horses ran wild. It didn't matter they were double-masked, twice-vaxxed, once-boosted, and keeping strict quarantine. It didn't matter that in the last decade of the last century they made a pilgrimage from Paris to Lourdes where strong young French workingmen, scented with sweat and Gauloises and the odor of sanctity, wrapped the naked bodies of him and the Husband, the atheist, tight in sheets of rough white canvas and dunked them in the frigid pools of healing waters as "a preventative," he told the Husband, "against everything." He trusted the Virgin Mother more than God the Father. Standing wary in the long line of sick pilgrims from around the world, and thinking about pollution and microorganisms, they drank the miraculous Lourdes water from a spout dripping from a mossy rock, and, just in case, filled six souvenir vials that the Husband who was a good sport said, "Somehow miraculously evaporated as soon as we got home."

Covid hit them like a gun shot.

"No no no no no!" He was a Duchamp nude falling down a staircase. "No no no no!"

"See why I'm an atheist," said the Husband whose atheism was more comfort than the old lord's anguished doubts.

"If I'm dying, bring my typewriter to my bed. The portable Mam and Da gave me for Christmas when I was seventeen. Only you three ever loved me."

Covid is nuclear. His smooth laminar flow becoming disrupted turned turbulent. Covid variant BA.5 ambushed them before they recognized they had begun coughing. There had been two hundred and fifty-eight mass shootings in the first six months of 2022. And it was only June. It was the June when everyone was sick.

"Last week of June, 4 million new U. S. cases, 8500 die"
"550 million cases, 6 million deaths in 200 countries"

On D-Day, the sixth of June, the official first day of fire season, he choked at breakfast swallowing a salmon-oil gelatin capsule that lodged in his throat. It was the birthday of his younger brother, the gun-loving Vietnam veteran dead from Agent Orange, who when they were boys thought it hilarious to shoot him with random sniper shots from his BB gun. The Husband patted his back and fed him pieces of dry bread. He coughed for four days thinking of Tennessee Williams choking to death on the screw top of a nose spray bottle at the Hotel Elysée, his "Hotel Easy Lay," thinking of his Blanche who stepping off a streetcar at "Elysian Fields" declared she would die of eating an unwashed grape.

On the fifth day of coughing, he tested positive at Urgent Care. On the advice of Doctor Google he forced himself into self-quarantine to keep the Husband safe. The Covid bed is not a coital bed. For the first time in forty-three years, the Futon-Duvets each lay solo under the covers in the bedroom and the guest room sleeping single in double beds. When the Husband tested positive the next day, old Doctor Quack said in a video appointment there was no need to quarantine from each other, but he was too fevered and breathless and restless to be a good bed partner. His get-up-and-go had got up and gone. As you live so shall you die. He was being dragged through the knothole of a gloryhole.

Alone in his delirium in their arts-and-crafts bedroom darkened with Thomas Mann draperies stitched up by Luchino Visconti, he dissolved into the great movie queen Dirk Bogarde in *Death in Venice* dissolving into the grand queen Gustav von Aschenbach disintegrating on the sandy beach of the Hôtel des Bains into death sweats, isolated, alone, *nobody loves me*, abandoned, masked face melting, hair dye running, dying of plague in Venice to the rhapsodic exit music of Mahler's *Adagietto Symphony No. 5*.

Flaccid with Covid, he dreamed about his greatest hits. If this was curtains, he intended to direct the curtain call of men: the bully boys he forced to sing and dance in his musical-comedy, the beatnik poet in Greenwich Village, the football team of Father O'Kneel, Steve Sales, and the general infantry of the sex revolution, the nameless band of brothers he had trusted with his body. The fraternity of that twenty-year orgy had been so gorgeous a single teardrop diamond, all he had left, caught in his eye for them and for the City.

"Don't cry for me, San Francisco."

Unlike Sodom and Gomorrah doomed for refusing to welcome outsiders, San Francisco did not deserve to be destroyed by Covid because its hospitality had for years kept it an open City for immigrants, sojourners, and queer refugees from around the world. It takes a fishing village with an opera to raise a culture safe enough for a sporting man to learn everything intimate and existential and divine about another man and himself in brief encounters with no domestic worries about their unpaid bills and unwashed dishes. He had rarely balled anyone under thirty. They were all older and dead, even the ones on Facebook, but it wasn't his fault.

His old-school Catholicism cames back to him in fever dreams. Altar-boy hymns returned on his playlist. Monks murmuring the Gregorian chant of "Pange Lingua." Pavarotti and Sting singing "Panis Angelicus. Sinéad O'Connor keening the ancient Greek "Kyrie Eleison," "Lord Have Mercy," with Ireland banning hugs, handshakes, and songs around the wake of a corpse in an open coffin in Aunt Molly's parlor. The calming hum of four-voice polyphony in melodies composed at Notre Dame in the Middle Ages that he had last heard during evening mass at the Cathedral years before the fire that for one day eclipsed the infinite TV coverage of Trump threatening to dump busloads of desperate immigrants on sanctuary cities like San Francisco.

He and the Husband had gasped in horror at the live telecast of the inferno that capsized the cathedral's 300-foot spire, tall as a football field is long, crashing its 800 tons of wood and melting lead down through the vaulted stone ceiling into the sanctuary on the spot where the Husband had sat while the old lord knelt before the Nigerian priest who placed the body and blood of Christ on his tongue.

He was glad they'd traveled when they still could. He took comfort in that marvelous June marking him turning seventy on their final trip to Europe in 2009 when they had the stamina to march with their video camera toward the Bastille in the Paris Pride Parade with thousands of Rainbow Parisians behind Liza Minnelli, *Quelle chance!*, striking *Cabaret* poses, dancing on a float shouting "Freedom!" He lay in bed offering his sufferings up for his own sins and the sins of the whole world uncertain whether his offer was like Saint Liza's "hands of a nun" prayer or camp.

"I am the Alpha and the Omicron."

Those who don't learn from adversity are fools. His first seven sick days were a week of repertory performances directed by Julian Beck and Judith Malina. On the Summer Solstice, his birthday, he turned eighty-three and heard the ghost of his ancient Mam telling him he was too young to die. He willed himself to feel better to re-set his age. He read that the first person to live to 150 was already born. He powered up thinking of the doomed voyager Vivien Leigh on the classic movie channel struggling on set with her own health, struggling on screen with fading youth, trapped on-board in her final film *Ship of Fools*. Forever Miss Scarlett and Miss DuBois and Mrs. Stone, she thrilled him when suddenly breaking out alone dancing in a deserted passage-way, she danced a dying flapper's last *danse macabre*, a comic "Charleston," flaming youth defying depression and death. He decided to put on his big-boy pants, get out of bed, call the dentist, prepare supper, take care of the Husband, and, like a good queen, defy the stars. He did not want to be sick or die in the worst room of any hotel.

That June after a two-year pause the Pride Parade re-turned to San Francisco. They sat together on a loveseat re-cliner watching a broadcast panel of drag queens and activists anchoring the coverage with camp commentary streaming live on TV. When the Grand Marshall float led by a roaring escort of Dykes on Bikes rolled on screen, they felt a sudden rush of *bonhomie* for the VIP riding atop the decorated plat-form, a transgender person, a rainbow warrior, a survivor standing tall, waving, reigning on the parade, clothed with the sun, with the moon under their feet, and on their head a crown of twelve stars. Was it a sign from heaven of life re-turning in a new normal? Over the City's Solstice skyline of vacant high rises and recumbent neighborhoods, Mercury, Venus, Mars, Jupiter, and Saturn shone in an alignment not seen since 1864 during the first Civil War.

Under that urban sky, unmasked millennials and Gen-Z zoomers, the next generation coming to power, self-ab-sorbed new tech immigrants oblivious to the City's past and paroxysms, carpetbaggers profiting from pandemic ruin, ex-ploiting downturns, raising start-up money, earning stock, renting condos in Victorian homes gay men once owned and restored, navigating a gender-fluid GPS history of their own identities, gathered on sidewalks by the entrances to gay bars and straight restaurants, drinking and smoking unmasked, swiping left on Tinder, eating *alfresco* in curbside dining sheds that were no threat to the sidewalk café terraces of Paris, no longer applauding healthcare workers, no longer looking up at the heavens, staring into their phones, downloading digital pop stars on TikTok, ignoring the analog crescent moon of Ishtar, the Goddess of Arabia, rising over their entitled little heads between Mars, the God of War, and Venus, the Goddess of Love, and not giving a shit.

24
September Harvest Moon

The friend, the sodomite waiter serving the Black Leather Swans in Palm Springs, called and said, "I got monkeypox at a Pride pool party. The pain was excruciating and the self-loathing is worse."

"Why loathing?"

"I knew better, but I went anyway."

Some people who were lost will never be found, buried so deep in desert sands and ice sheets and crevasses and pollution and bullshit that they will never emerge from the shifting sand dunes or from the calving glaciers creeping out to an ocean of micro-plastic bits floating under a sky of space junk.

"So when are you and good-old-what's-his name moving to Palm Springs? San Francisco is so over."

"Really? You really think Covid is stronger than the 1906 earthquake and fire?"

His love affair with San Francisco would never end. He was happy he and the Husband would rest together forever in the Columbarium of the Futon-Duvets in Grace Cathedral atop Nob Hill overlooking the Golden Gate.

"Queen Elizabeth II has died"
"Subvariant rise: BA.2.75, BA.2.75.2, BA.4.6, and BF.7"
"How school shootings affect kid survivors"
"Putin turns 70 in bunker with finger on nuclear button"
"Activist pelts King Charles, Queen Camilla with eggs"
"Hurricane Ian obliterates parts of Florida"
"Florida gay couple shoot selves outside destroyed home"
"U.S. lab creates super-Covid with 80% kill rate"

“Worst September for stocks since 2002”
“Harry & Meghan bitter battle with William & Kate”
“Proud Boys leader pleads guilty”
“Viral bird flu pandemic could soon jump to humans”
“West plans to avoid panic if Russia nukes Ukraine”
“Europe Covid spike means fast-moving U.S. winter wave”
“Unattractive more likely to wear masks post-Covid”
“Progressives fight West Hollywood pioneers over future”
“The rise of Trumpism without Trump”
“Woke San Francisco ghost town worse than it looks”

The old lord stood in the doorway of their castle, masked, ready to make his *sortie spectaculaire* out into the sun on their deck because dramatic exits, back-of-hand-pressed-to-forehead, are better in French. “I haven’t had this much fun making a public appearance since the cast of *Hair* invited the audience to dance nude on stage.”

“We have a two-o’clock appointment,” the Husband said, “for the new Omicron booster.”

“What are you doing with that video camera?”

“Surprise! It’s the new drone camera we wanted to order.”

“Oh, God. Another eye in the sky.”

“Are you ready for your close-up?”

“What’s real?” he asked. “What’s acting? Why have we filmed ourselves for years? What’s life performed for a camera? What will artificial-intelligence do to us? Are we the Futon-Duvets or not? We die. They will live forever. Is this my swan song? The irony of the camera is no one’s watching you because no one cares.”

Cameras change people into performers. When there’s a neighborhood shooting, news reporters interview witnesses playacting sound effects into the TV camera: “Me and my fiancé heard Pop! Pop! Pop!” He preferred observational cameras that did not change behavior.

"I'm watching you," the younger lover said launching the drone. "We shall have these moments to remember."

The older lover, the voyeur, the observer observed, felt the spy-power of the eight-ounce 4K camera hovering in front of his face with its running timecode capturing him on the threshold of whatever would happen next. Hope sobered his Covid Blues. "I'll drive. Let me drive." His confidence was rising like a cocky adolescent turning sweet sixteen with his first driver's license, the keys to daddy's car, and a condom in his wallet. "I haven't driven in three years."

His whole life he had defied what he was expected to do. Bully boys straight and gay taught him to punch back. Drought taught him to drink deep of the Pierian spring of life. Firestorms taught him sometimes the only way out of a fire is into the frying pan of a flaming life.

He played to the flying camera the Husband was circling around his head like a hummingbird. Who doesn't want to win an Oscar? He threw his scarf around his neck like Isadora Duncan, born in San Francisco, making a grand exit in the Roaring Twenties in the South of France, speeding off in her gigolo's convertible waving with a wild flourish of her long red silk scarf that caught in the rear wheels of the Bugatti and broke her neck.

He did his dialogue. "Nobody puts baby in a corner."

"Calm down. This is just a quick out and back for the vax."

Shot from above by the drone, the old lord walked out across the deck into the new imitation of life. "Let us go then, you and I, before we're laid out like patients ventilated on a table. I'm not breaking quarantine until there's a once-a-year shot like the flu vaccine."

In this sad pandemic, is there a cycle of grief that resolves itself, or is it a circle of grief that never ends? And you just get on with it careful as you can.

He put on his sunglasses. "Back to the masquerade."

The Husband banking the aerial shot higher above his lover's head said, "The show must go on."

The old lord said, "Should we buy radiation pills if Putin nukes the Golden Gate Bridge? Or just go straight to cyanide?"

"What's that new car coming up the drive?"

"Did you order something for delivery?"

The Husband flew the drone down to peer through the windshield. "It's Frau Pancake and the purebreds."

"What the fuck does she want?"

www.ingramcontent.com/pod-product-compliance
Lightning Source LLC
Chambersburg PA
CBHW030808190726
48285CB00003B/1080